BLACKMAILING MR. BOSSMAN

BILLIONAIRE HEISTS #2

ANNA HACKETT

Blackmailing Mr. Bossman

Published by Anna Hackett

Copyright 2021 by Anna Hackett

Cover by RBA Designs

Cover image by Wander Aguiar

Edits by Tanya Saari

ISBN (ebook): 978-1-922414-31-1

ISBN (paperback): 978-1-922414-32-8

WHAT READERS ARE SAYING ABOUT ANNA'S ACTION ROMANCE

Heart of Eon - Romantic Book of the Year (Ruby) winner 2020

Cyborg - PRISM Award Winner 2019

Edge of Eon and Mission: Her Protection - Romantic Book of the Year (Ruby) finalists 2019

Unfathomed and Unmapped - Romantic Book of the Year (Ruby) finalists 2018

Unexplored – Romantic Book of the Year (Ruby) Novella Winner 2017

Return to Dark Earth – One of Library Journal's Best E-Original Books for 2015 and two-time SFR Galaxy Awards winner

At Star's End – One of Library Journal's Best E-Original Romances for 2014

The Phoenix Adventures – SFR Galaxy Award Winner for Most Fun New Series and "Why Isn't This a Movie?" Series

Beneath a Trojan Moon – SFR Galaxy Award Winner and RWAus Ella Award Winner

Hell Squad – SFR Galaxy Award for best Post-Apocalypse for Readers who don't like Post-Apocalypse

Sign up for my VIP mailing list and get your *free box set* containing three action-packed romances.

Visit here to get started: www.annahackett.com

GOING TO GET HIM BACK

Aspen

Cell phone pressed to one ear, I slipped the high heel on, hopping a little to keep my balance. "I'm sorry, Mr. McGillis, I'm already working a case right now and I'm *really* busy."

"That's too bad." The older man blew out a breath that echoed down the line. "My baby girl's man is cheating on her, and I want her free of the asshole. He's put her through hell. Warned her not to marry him."

"I'm really sorry to hear that." I scanned my closet floor for the other shoe. *Where the hell was it?* I stared longingly at my favorite pair of Nikes.

"When I asked around the neighborhood for a PI to help us, your name came up so many times. They said 'you need to talk to Aspen Chandler. Girl's a hard worker and gets the job done.' That's what everyone told me."

A little kernel of warmth bloomed in my chest. "I'm so happy to hear that, and I really am sorry I don't have time to help you right now." No, I officially had zero spare time. I was working a tough case, and had my best friend's husband to save. I blew out a breath. Right now, I felt like I was juggling a hundred balls in the air and at any second, they could all tumble down on my head. "Look, I know a few other private investigators I can recommend. Any of them would do a great job and help your daughter."

"That would be great, Aspen." Relief drenched the man's voice. "I appreciate it."

"Sure thing." I spied the other black heel. "I'll send you a message with the names. Good luck, Mr. McGillis."

"Thanks, Aspen."

Ending the call, I snagged the shoe and slipped it on. I could barely walk in these heels, but each day I worked this case, I was getting a little better at it. I just prayed I wouldn't break an ankle. The Manolo Blahniks were sexy as hell—I'd snagged them for a song on sale—they just weren't my usual footwear.

As a private investigator, I was usually conducting surveillance or tracking down missing persons. Hard to run or climb a fence in heels. Unfortunately, I had to run more than I liked.

I straightened and took a second to absorb the peace and harmony of my bedroom. It was my own little sanctuary, away from the chaos of the outside world.

When my father's parents had died, they'd left their apartment, in an old pre-war building in Kips Bay, to me. I'd been touched and humbled. I'd tried to see them both as much as I could, but it never felt like enough.

So, I'd gotten an apartment, and taken over the mortgage they'd taken out to cover their medical bills, but it was still a great deal. There was no way I could have afforded a place in Manhattan, otherwise.

I'd slowly renovated it room by room. I'd painted the apartment in crisp white, with touches of wood and green. I'd sanded and refinished the hardwood floors myself, and I'd filled the place with plants. I couldn't cook, but I was pretty proud of my green thumb.

A fiddle leaf fig sat in one corner of my bedroom, its large leaves a waxy, deep green. A bushy fern was perched under the window, and I had a row of smaller plants in pots resting on a shelf on the wall opposite the bed.

My bed had a padded, gray headboard, and was covered in comfy, luxurious bedding. Since I spent a lot of time following cheating spouses, or doing surveillance on insurance cheats, I liked my apartment—or at least my bedroom—to be an oasis of calm.

"Juno, you drank the last of the juice!" The screech came from the kitchen.

"No, I didn't."

"You did!"

Ah, yes, I had so much peace and serenity when I had my younger sisters living with me.

I headed out to the kitchen to attempt to stop the fight before it devolved into name calling, hair pulling, or worse.

The design of the apartment meant that my room was on one side of the living area, while the twins shared the other room on the other side. It gave us a modicum of privacy. Unfortunately, we had to share a bathroom, which wasn't ideal.

"You're such a douchnozzle," Briar snapped.

"And you're a dickladle."

Too late. The twins loved combining words to come up with weird curses.

"Hey, keep it down," I called out. I followed the scent of coffee straight to the coffeepot. "Just put juice on the shopping list on the fridge."

The twins swiveled to face me. Briar and Juniper were identical—five foot eight, athletic figures, blonde hair. It was obvious we were sisters, since I was blonde as well, but I was a couple of inches shorter and a little curvier. They'd both played volleyball at high school, and Briar still played at college.

The twins were nineteen going on thirty-five, and both attending college. Juniper was studying business at Columbia, and Briar was pre-med at NYU.

Juniper, who went by Juno, looked me up and down, then put her fingers in her mouth and wolf whistled.

I rolled my eyes. I was wearing a fitted, long, black skirt, a white shirt with a ruffle at the neckline, and a camel-colored, three-quarter-length coat. It wasn't my usual work attire, but for this case, I was undercover.

"You look hot, especially in those come-fuck-me shoes." Briar waggled her eyebrows, then hitched herself up on the small kitchen island. "I'd bang you."

"Thank you...I think." I poured a coffee, inhaling the smell of my strong, earthy Robusta. Then I popped a piece of bread into the toaster. "I need to get going, or I'll be late for my undercover job." I also needed to meet my client, who happened to be my high school best friend, before I got to the office.

At the thought of Erica, my chest constricted.

"I like this particular job of yours, since you get to dress up." Juno waggled her eyebrows in the exact same way her twin had. "It's a *huge* improvement on your collection of jeans, jeans, and jeans."

Briar stole my coffee and took a sip. "And T-shirts, T-shirts, T-shirts."

"And Nikes, Nikes, Nikes."

I needed to stop them before they got on a roll. "I don't need to dress like a fashion plate for my usual jobs."

"So, where *are* you working?" Briar asked.

"That's classified." I stole my coffee back. "Don't you two have classes?"

"Later," Juno said.

"You work too hard," Briar said quietly.

My head whipped up and I met her gaze. "What?"

"You work too hard. Take too many cases."

Juno nodded. "I know some of them can't always pay."

I cleared my throat. "I like helping people—"

"Our father was a dickweasel," Briar said. "But that doesn't mean you have to make up for his crimes."

I straightened. "That's *not* what I'm doing. I like my work. I have a mortgage to pay, and two annoying sisters to support."

They both rolled their eyes, but thankfully dropped the subject. My toast popped up, and I quickly slathered it with peanut butter and jelly. I glanced at my watch and winced.

Dammit. I had ten minutes to meet Erica at a coffee shop around the corner. "I have to run."

I gulped more coffee and took a bite of my toast. I raced around shoving my things in my bag. After I'd wolfed down the rest of my toast, I brushed my teeth, and swiped some gloss on my lips.

"Bye," I yelled, opening the front door.

"Bye!"

"Be safe."

I smiled as I took the central stairs. Life with my sisters was always noisy and colorful. I wouldn't trade it for anything.

A door opened. "Aspen?"

I spun and saw Mrs. Kerber in her doorway, with her fluffy, white cat tucked under her arm. Mrs. Kerber was a widow and lived one floor below me.

"Hey, Mrs. Kerber." I glanced at the cat. "Hi, Milo."

The cat glared at me with evil, blue eyes. I couldn't ever shake the feeling that Milo was plotting my murder, or possibly world domination.

"You look pretty today, dear," Mrs. Kerber said. "How are those lovely sisters of yours?"

Luckily, Mrs. Kerber didn't always wear her hearing aid, or she'd hear that lovely and the twins didn't always match up.

"They're great. Doing well at school."

"Wonderful." Mrs. Kerber stroked Milo's head. "Aspen, Skittles got out again. Could you help? I'm worried about him."

I sighed. I didn't have time for this.

The old woman watched me, pleading in her eyes. I

knew she had trouble navigating the stairs because of her vertigo. I smiled. "Don't worry, I'll find him."

"Oh, thank you, dear. You're such a good girl."

That was me, Aspen Chandler, good girl. I often took small cases from neighbors, and they paid me with baked goods, or by doing odd jobs around my apartment. Mr. Billings around the corner had replumbed my bathroom, in return for me surveilling one of his employees, who was claiming he'd hurt his back on the job. I'd gotten some great snaps of the guy at the gym, and him helping his friend move house, and snagged myself brand-new pipes.

I hoofed it down the stairs. I suspected I knew where Skittles was.

Sure enough, the yellow cockatiel was perched on a ledge in the building entry, waiting for someone to open the front door so he could make a bid for freedom. I was certain the bird was trying to escape Milo. If Milo watched me with a scary look of disdain, the cat watched Skittles like he was starving and dinner was served.

"Come on, Skittles."

After I'd retrieved the bird and returned him to Mrs. Kerber, I was now officially late. I pulled out my personal cell and tapped in a quick text to Erica.

Then I hit the sidewalk and jogged. *Please don't break an ankle.*

By the time I reached the coffee shop, I was huffing and puffing.

It was a tiny place, and popular. I pushed through the crowd, and spied Erica sitting at a table at the back.

My friend noticed me and shot to her feet. "Aspen."

My heart clenched. Erica Knox was a coppery-redhead, with milky-white skin covered in freckles. Usually she was smiling, with a twinkle in her eyes. In high school, she'd always been giggling. She'd been one of my closest friends, after I'd been forced to change schools at fourteen. She'd made school bearable for me.

There was no sign of that smile or giggle now. She looked pale, drawn, and tired. Huge, dark circles underscored her blue eyes. Like me, she wore office attire, and I noted that her belted blue dress was a little loose. She'd lost weight these last few weeks.

"Hey." I took her hand and squeezed. "Sorry I'm late."

Erica swallowed. "Do you...uh, want a coffee or anything?"

"I'm fine." We sat. "How are you holding up?"

"I...I..." Tears welled in Erica's eyes.

I leaned across the table. "We're going to get him back, E. I promise."

Erica nodded. "I know. I just worry." Her voice dropped to a whisper. "It's been almost a month."

Four weeks ago, Erica's new husband, Jake, had failed to come home from work. She'd gone to the cops, who'd told her to wait. That he'd probably turn up. Maybe marriage had freaked him out and he'd gone off to clear his head.

Then she'd gotten a message.

We have your husband. Do as we say, and you'll get him back alive. Do not contact the police or he's dead. If you don't do exactly as we say...

Erica had come to me, panicked and on the verge of a breakdown.

I'd suggested she go to the police, but she'd lost it. Then I'd told her to wait and see what Jake's abductors demanded.

Meanwhile, behind the scenes, I'd gotten busy doing some quiet digging and pulling in a few favors. I'd discovered who'd taken Jake.

Nexus.

Just the name set my gut churning.

Nexus was a smart, cunning group of white-collar criminals who specialized in corporate espionage, blackmail of wealthy business people and politicians, and a dash of embezzlement and corporate fraud. They kept their shit tight, took the time to plan their cons, and picked big targets.

What they wanted from Erica was neither quick or easy, and each day, I saw it wear on my friend.

Erica was a manager who worked in human resources for the Kensington Group—a large, multi-billion-dollar construction and property development company. Nexus had asked her to keep tabs on the company's owner and CEO. To feed them information on his schedule and movements.

Their next target was Liam Kensington—one of the infamous Billionaire Bachelors of New York.

They didn't come much bigger.

"Nexus haven't sent me any instructions for days," Erica whispered.

"Don't worry, they've been dealing with me." As of three weeks ago, I'd become her stand-in with the shadowy white-collar crime gang. "I've been getting texts. They've been checking that I'm in place."

After Erica had come to me, I knew I had to help her. She was barely holding it together.

And I had extra incentive.

Every single thing I'd learned about Nexus had turned my stomach. They'd pulled off a huge insurance fraud earlier in the year. They'd destroyed the livelihoods of hundreds of families.

I smiled sharply. They were going down. I knew better than anyone the devastation that heartless criminals like these left behind. I'd lived and breathed it as a teenager.

I lifted my chin. The cold, greedy assholes who hid in plain sight and believed they had the right to everyone else's money were done. *Finito.*

I'd activated an old alias of mine and dropped some breadcrumbs. Nexus had swiftly taken the bait. They thought I was a shady lawyer called Penn Channing, who knew my way around some not-so-legal dealings, and liked to make a quick buck.

Barely a week after making contact with them, they'd ordered me to go undercover at Kensington Group. They'd told me they felt their asset at the company—I wanted to punch them for calling Erica an asset—wasn't solid enough to see through the plan. Erica had arranged for me to get hired as an assistant in the Marketing department.

I didn't know the big picture yet. Nexus was good at only revealing bits of info to certain people.

Only Kristoff Doyle knew everything.

The leader of Nexus was a fifty-eight-year-old man with no past. I hadn't found out a single thing about him. Not even a clear photograph. He stayed in the shadows.

"You think Nexus is getting ready to move on Mr. Kensington?" Erica asked.

I nodded. "Doyle's moving pieces behind the scenes. I have no idea what he has on Kensington, but it can't be good."

I was now the proud owner of a thick dossier on the billionaire. As far as I could tell, Liam Kensington was what he seemed—thirty-five years old, handsome as sin, rich. He liked his women long and leggy. He had an American mother and a British father, and he'd been raised in London until his parents' bitter divorce. He had a slew of half siblings from his father's second and third marriages.

While Liam Kensington was clean, his father was not. Rupert Kensington had been implicated in plenty of dirty deals. He also kept some bad company, but he'd never been charged with anything.

Word was that Liam didn't speak to the elder Kensington. He'd gone to Harvard, and then stayed in the U.S. He'd met his best friends—Zane Roth and Maverick Rivera—and the three of them had all gone on to huge success. The three billionaire bachelors of New York. Although according to the latest society pages, it appeared that Zane Roth was happily taken.

Liam Kensington also happened to be the sexiest, most beautiful man I'd ever laid eyes on.

I'd caught a couple of glimpses of him in the halls of the Kensington Group head office over the last two weeks, but I'd seen him up close and personal at a recent charity event at his newest nightclub.

I barely suppressed a shiver, but there was nothing I could do about the clench low in my belly. Yes, Liam Kensington looked like some god come to life, deigning to visit the mere mortals.

He was over six feet tall, with a long, lean swimmer's body, and burnished-gold hair. He wore a suit in a way that made a woman want to whimper. And his face...

I'd never thought a man could be beautiful, but still masculine. But Kensington managed it, and was often at the top of all the lists of the most handsome, wealthy bachelors.

"Aspen?"

I blinked. *Crap.* "Sorry, just thinking." And totally not daydreaming about how gorgeous Liam Kensington was. "Did they send you a video today?"

Erica nodded and showed me her phone.

The grainy, black-and-white footage of Jake in a cell, lying on a narrow bunk and staring at the wall, was only a few seconds long. He shifted a little, and I studied the time stamp. It was dated this morning.

"He's alive, Erica. You keep doing what you're doing, and I'll keep working my end."

Erica pulled out a Kleenex and dabbed her eyes. "Nexus promised that as soon as they get what they want from Mr. Kensington, they'll release Jake."

I gripped her hand and prayed Nexus held up their end of the bargain. Behind the scenes, I'd been noting down Nexus locations in the hope of finding where they were holding the man, but I was coming up empty-handed. "We're going to get him back."

"Thank you, Aspen. You're the best. I...would have fallen apart without you."

I squeezed her hand. "You're stronger than you think. Now, I need to go and be Penn Channing. You know, I rock at being a marketing assistant."

Erica gave a watery laugh. "Something tells me you'd rock at anything you try."

I winked at her. "I might stay until Christmas. I hear Kensington gives a good bonus."

Another small laugh. "He does."

"Remember, if you see me at the office, I'm Penn, and we don't know each other."

"Got it."

I hurried to the subway and headed to the Kensington Group building in lower Manhattan. It was a huge spire of glass that Kensington had built several years ago. He had several construction projects on the go around New York. I suspected the man owned half of the city.

As soon as I got to my desk, I was sucked into work and meetings. The upside of being undercover was I was getting a second paycheck, at least.

I didn't see Erica, and I also didn't see Kensington.

Bummer. I really wouldn't mind another look at him.

My head was still humming with thoughts of Nexus. They were getting ready to make their move on Kensington. I could feel it growing like a thunderstorm.

What the hell did they have on him?

It didn't matter. My priority was seeing this through and getting Jake Knox back home safely.

Finally, the office started to empty out and my stomach grumbled. I rose. Time to head home. My feet were killing me, and I had a desperate need for some chocolate.

In the elevator, I checked my phone. I had a missed call from my mom, and I also had several texts from my sisters.

I'm not cooking tonight.

That was from Juniper.

It's your turn, Juno. You can't weasel out.

That was Briar.

I'm tired. And I dumped Jason today. He's a twatwaffle.

Instantly, Briar morphed into loving, supportive sister.

Juno xxx. He is a twatwaffle, and a pisswizard. Never liked him.

I know. You made that very obvious, Bri.

I tapped in a message.

Juno, sorry about Jason. Need I remind you two that you live with me, rent-free, and the only expectation I have is that you cook dinner?

I sucked in the kitchen and I often worked odd hours. Having the twins cook was a huge help.

Fine. I'll make some pasta.

I could almost hear Juno's dramatic sigh all the way across Manhattan.

By the time I made it to the subway, my feet were really killing me. When I got on the train, I squished in with everyone else heading home, and knew there was no way I'd nab a seat. I promised myself I'd soak my feet when I got home.

I got off at 28th Street Station and took a convoluted path home. I didn't think Nexus were watching me, but there was no way I was leading them to my apartment. Satisfied that I wasn't being followed, I gave into my growing chocolate craving, and stopped at the small convenience store near my building. Neon signs flashed in the window, for beer, an ATM, and the lotto.

"Hey, Mr. Cavonis," I called out.

"Aspen," the older man replied from behind the counter. "How you been?"

"Busy."

"Haven't seen those sisters of yours for a while."

"Lucky you."

He laughed.

Navigating the cramped store, I grabbed an armful of different chocolates. I had a secret addiction to Belgian, Swiss, and some of the artisanal French chocolate, but I could rarely afford the good stuff. I usually ordered myself a box of truffles online for my birthday.

I dumped my selection of Hershey's, Snickers, 3 Musketeers, and Twix bars on the counter.

Mr. Cavonis' bushy eyebrows rose. "You having a party?"

"Nope. Wait a second—" I raced back for some Reese's bars.

The door jangled. I'd just grabbed some more choco-lates when I heard Mr. Cavonis gasp.

I spun. A man in jeans and a gray hoodie stood at the

counter, holding a knife up. "Empty the register! I want *all* your money."

Mr. Cavonis was frozen. I edged closer.

"Move, old man," the thief yelled. "Now!"

The newcomer was probably late twenties, white skin with freckles, and a few wisps of brown hair sticking out from under the hood. He was shaking a little, and there were beads of perspiration on his upper lip. I quietly dropped the candy bars back into their display box.

"Oh, my God." I injected panic into my voice, moving closer.

He spun to face me, the switchblade aimed my way. "Stop moving!"

His pupils were dilated. High on something. "Please don't hurt me." There, that was a pretty good impression of a terrified woman.

He looked away. *Yes, that's right. Just dismiss me as a hysterical woman.*

"Give me the cash!"

I hiked my tight skirt up to my thighs, and moved. I landed a hard chop to the man's arm. The knife hit the linoleum, and the thief yelped. I gave a hard front kick to his belly, my sharp heel digging into his gut.

Huh, they did come in handy after all. Who knew?

With a cry, the man flew backward into a display of cookies, sending packets spilling everywhere.

I grabbed some zip ties out of my handbag. A good investigator never left home without them. My Glock 43 was also tucked in there. I had a concealed-carry permit, and I tried to get to the firing range at least once a month, but I only pulled the weapon out if I really, really needed it.

I flipped the crying, struggling thief over and tied his hands behind his back.

"You're lucky I didn't punch you," I said. "I'm tired, stressed, my feet hurt, and you got between me and my chocolate."

The man made a strangled sound.

I straightened. "Mr. Cavonis, did you call 9-1-1?"

"Yes, Aspen." The man's voice was shaky. "They're on their way. Thank you."

I nabbed a Hershey's bar, opened it, and took a large bite. *Mmm.* "What do I owe you for the chocolate?"

The storeowner managed a smile. "Nothing. They're on the house."

Well, at least one part of my day was looking up.

My burner phone beeped, and when I saw the message, my mood plummeted.

Be ready for instructions tomorrow. We're ready to move on the target.

2

LOVE PHEROMONES

Liam

Liam Kensington rounded the corner and lengthened his stride. Ahead, he saw the end of the race, with banners flapping in the air. Either side of him, illuminated by bright lights, the crowds cheered.

Blood pumped through his veins and his chest heaved. He was almost at the end of the six-mile, evening charity run in Central Park. He'd already made a large donation and had sponsored the event—for Hope for the Warriors, a fantastic charity that supported wounded veterans.

The crowd's cheers intensified and he glanced back.

His two best friends—Zane Roth and Maverick River—were gaining on him. Zane was pumping his arms, the same look on his face that he got when he was brokering a multi-million-dollar deal. Mav's dark brows were drawn together, and he looked fierce as he powered through the final stretch.

Liam picked up the pace. He crossed the finish line, his friends just steps behind him.

"I almost caught you, Kensington," Mav said. He was big and dark-haired, and was more often than not scowling. He had the personality of a bear. Liam had liked him from the first day they'd met. He'd been a refreshing change after growing up in the very proper, very posh London social scene.

Liam sucked in some deep breaths. "Almost doesn't cut it, Rivera."

Zane leaned over, hands on his thighs. "Hell, I need to get back on the treadmill."

Mav snorted. "Because most of your exercise of late involves a certain sexy brunette."

Zane grinned. "Hell, yeah."

The three of them walked toward the water station. The crowd cheered, and near the temporary fence, several women were screaming at them.

"Marry me, Liam!"

"I'll have your babies, Maverick."

"Zane, I'm a better girlfriend!"

When the press had given the three of them the name the billionaire bachelors of New York, Liam had wanted to punch someone. He managed to dredge up a smile and waved.

They reached the water stand where race volunteers were handing out bottles. A perky blonde circled the table. "Here you go, Liam."

He took the bottle and nodded. She grabbed his hand and turned the bottle so he could see where she'd written what he assumed was her phone number. She winked at him before returning to her work.

Liam stifled a sigh and cracked the lid off the bottle.

Next to him, Zane waggled his eyebrows. "She's cute."

Liam waved a hand and drank some water. That woman didn't know anything about him, except for his net worth. He was...a little tired of it all.

"Mr. Kensington."

Turning, he saw a tall, lean man in a Hope for the Warriors jacket waving at him. Tim was the charity race organizer.

"Well done on your run." Tim pushed his glasses up the bridge of his nose, then held out a hand.

Liam shook the man's hand. "Thanks. The event's been great. It looks like a great turn out."

"All thanks to your sponsorship and support." Tim's eyes gleamed behind his glasses. "Thank you for your amazing donation." He looked over Liam's shoulder at the others. "And your friends as well."

"Happy to help a charity that does such great work." Once Tim left, Liam turned, just in time to see a black-haired woman in dark jeans and a red coat race toward Zane.

His friend's face lit up. He snatched up the woman and hauled her off her feet for a kiss.

Monroe pressed her hands to Zane's shoulders. "Hey, you're all sweaty, Roth."

"Don't care, Wildcat. It's been too long since I kissed you."

"I gave you a kiss before the race."

"Definitely too long." After that, Zane got busy kissing the hell out of his girlfriend.

Monroe O'Connor had blasted into Zane's life recently, and turned it upside down.

The locksmith—and daughter of a thief—had a wayward brother who'd landed himself in debt to the wrong people. Very wrong people. It'd set Zane and Monroe on a collision course.

The two had ended up saving each other—and her brother—and generated enough steam to power Long Island.

It was also clear that they were hopelessly in love.

Liam had no illusions about love. He'd watched his father blow through women his entire life. He'd watched his mother harden her heart after she'd had it broken more times than he could count, and then introduced him to her younger and younger boyfriends.

Since Liam had found success, women threw themselves at him so often it got tiring.

But as he stared at Zane and Monroe, he felt a sharp pang in his chest. *Bloody hell.* He was jealous.

Suddenly, standing there in the middle of Central Park, pulse still elevated and running gear soaked with sweat, he realized that he wanted a Monroe. He wanted a smart, funny woman who was totally in love with him the way Monroe loved Zane. And the woman did love Zane, not his wealth or the trappings of it.

"You okay, Kensington?"

Liam glanced at Mav. "Sure." He took another swig of water.

He hadn't had a relationship longer than a month or

two in a long time. He loved women, in all their many shapes and varieties, and he'd indulged that. When he looked in the mirror, he was afraid he'd start to see his father.

The water curdled in his gut.

Rupert chased anything in a skirt. Since he'd separated from his third wife, there had been an endless parade of young women. Liam dragged in a breath. Hell, it had probably been going on since before his separation.

Liam had no desire to be anything remotely like his father.

But one thing you couldn't escape was the blood in your veins.

"Next race, I'm beating your British ass," Mav said.

Liam shook off his thoughts. "Not bloody likely, but you're welcome to try. Maybe we'll add a side bet. The loser has to double their donation to the charity."

Mav nodded. "Deal."

They both looked at Zane and Monroe. The pair were still kissing.

"Those two ooze love pheromones," Liam said.

Mav grunted.

Liam smiled. "Careful or you might catch the love bug."

"*Never*," Mav growled.

Mav had fallen for a pretty, young thing in college. He'd been on the verge of making serious money after the sale of some fancy computer chip. Needless to say, the young lady had been a very clever gold-digger. Mav had gotten burned, and since then, he fucked, but let no woman get close. Ever.

Liam watched Monroe stroke Zane's cheek.

For some reason, he thought of a certain blonde who worked in his marketing department.

He squelched that thought. He barely knew Penn Channing, and she worked for him. End of story. She'd attended a fundraiser Monroe and Zane had organized a few days ago. When a man had gotten violent, Penn had taken the guy down without batting an eyelid.

And Liam couldn't seem to stop thinking about her.

"You want that?" Mav tilted his head at Zane and Monroe.

"Maybe." Liam straightened. "But I'd have to find the right woman first. She needs to be beautiful, talented, smart, funny—"

"Jesus, you're a perfectionist snob sometimes, Kensington."

"I like quality." Liam sniffed. "Nothing wrong with that."

"Like those damn Saville Row suits you collect."

"British tailors are exceptional at what they do. That's just a fact."

Mav snorted. "Come on, Brit. I'll buy you a drink. Next time, when I win the race, you'll owe me one."

Liam shook his head. Mav hated losing. He glanced at the crowd and saw some photographers. Most were busy snapping shots of Zane and Monroe. It was big news that one of the billionaires was off the market.

That's when Liam noticed that one of the photographers had a giant camera lens pointed his way. Not unusual. He was used to photographers, and tolerated the press, even when more often than not they were a pain in his ass. This man had a dark-green ball cap pulled low over his face, and no press pass around his neck.

"Hey, lovebirds," Mav said. "Quit making out and let's get a drink."

Zane discreetly shot Mav the finger, but set a smiling Monroe down.

When Liam glanced back at the photographer, the man was gone. Liam straightened. "Let's drink."

Aspen

"What did you do to my mascara, Briar?"

"Nothing. I didn't touch it! I used your eyeliner though. And your blush. And your bronzer."

"Stay out of my makeup!"

I rolled over and squinted at my alarm clock. It was still early, but the twins were up, gracing me with their morning serenity.

Stretching, I started to roll over, but then I remembered that text from Nexus. Today, they were finally going to make a move on Kensington.

I didn't know the man, but for an insanely wealthy billionaire, he seemed like a good guy. His staff all enjoyed working at Kensington Group. I hoped he wasn't really an asshole.

I heard more screeching from my sisters' bedroom, and with a sigh, I rose and snagged my robe. I wrapped the dark-blue fabric around myself and headed out to the kitchen.

Hurrying through my breakfast and morning routine, I tuned out the twins' arguments. After I'd showered, changed, and called out goodbyes to Briar and Juno, I caught a cab to the Kensington Group office. I could have walked and gotten the subway, but my feet still didn't love me. Even after I'd soaked them last night. I wasn't wearing those black heels again.

As I settled into the back seat, my cell phone rang— my personal one—and when I pulled it out, my mom's name flashed up on the display.

"Hi, Mom. I only have a minute."

"Hey, baby. You're always so busy. You need to relax more." Her tone was soft and sweet. That described Joanna Chandler perfectly.

"I'm working on a case for a friend."

My mom lived upstate, in the small town of Beacon. She worked as an artist and sold just enough paintings to scrape by. She generally didn't stress about anything, and believed the Universe would provide.

I wished I could not stress, but someone had to pay the bills.

I'd been fourteen when my father had gotten involved in a financial scandal. He'd been caught up in a Ponzi scheme that had cost our family, and others, everything. He'd been arrested and gone to jail, and my gentle, flighty mother had been helpless. The money was gone, the large family home gone, too, and the family reputation shattered. My mom had fallen apart.

The twins had been four. Someone had needed to pick up the pieces.

"How are my babies?" Mom asked.

"The twins are good. Busy. Noisy."

My mom laughed. It was a sweet, airy sound that always made me think of fairies. Sometimes Mom frustrated me to hell because she didn't always live in the real world, but I loved her.

"I'm hoping to see them soon. There's an art show in the city that I want to take them to."

"They'll love to see you."

"And I know there's no point in asking you to come."

I'd rather watch paint dry. "You know art isn't my thing."

My mother released a gusty sigh. "I don't know how I ended up with such a practical child."

Because I had to grow up and be the adult at fourteen.

I shoved the old emotions down. "It'll be nice to see you." And it meant I'd have to give my mom my bed and sleep on the pull-out couch. I stifled a sigh. I also felt a niggle. "Is there a reason you're calling, Mom?"

My mother was quiet for a moment. "Ronnie left."

Hell. Her latest man was gone. That meant she was low on money.

I closed my eyes. "I'm sorry, Mom."

"It hadn't been working between us for a while." Another pause. "Could you just send me a few hundred dollars, Aspen? Until I sell my next few paintings."

"Sure, Mom, I can send you some money."

"You're such a good girl, Aspen. Thank you. Today, okay?"

I blew out a breath. "Yes, I'll send it today."

"Thanks, Aspen. I love you."

"Love you, too." I tucked a strand of hair back and opened my banking app to make the transfer. As I put my phone away, I noticed the cab driver watching me in the rear-view mirror.

"Mommas are supposed to look after their kids, not kids looking after their mommas."

Great. Advice from a cab driver.

"Thanks." I paid and climbed out.

I hurried into the plush lobby of the Kensington Group building.

Inside was sleek and modern, with a touch of British charm. Light poured in through the walls of glass. The back wall was all shiny, gray tiles with a long reception desk. Large, colorful pieces of artwork hung on the walls, all showcasing the British countryside or portraits of who I assumed were kings and dukes of old.

But I had no time to study the paintings today. I thought of poor Jake, and my chest tightened. Erica was hanging on by a thread. I needed to see this through and help her get her husband back safely.

I took the elevator to the 52nd floor.

"There you are." Abigail, another assistant I'd been working with, rushed forward, looking harried. "Lisa needs you to sort this."

Abigail slapped a file at me, blowing her straight, black bangs out of her eyes. Lisa was our boss and the head of marketing.

"Take this to the executive level on the top floor, and get Mr. Kensington to sign it."

"Okay." I dumped my bag and coat at my desk.

"As in, sign it now," Abigail insisted. "His assistant,

Eleanor, is impossible to get past. Especially if you're young and gorgeous."

I raised a brow. I knew I had my strengths, but I didn't usually rate as gorgeous.

Abigail's nose wrinkled. "There's always some new hire or intern trying to wave their tits at Mr. Kensington."

I grimaced. "Really?"

Abigail shooed me. "Go. Need it signed yesterday."

I straightened my shoulders. "On it."

"And don't wave your tits."

"I don't...even know how to do that." I needed to make one detour, then I'd get that file signed, and get a chance to scope out Liam Kensington up close and personal.

Before I had to shatter his glossy, expensive world.

3

A MUCH BETTER OFFER

Liam

"I want a site visit organized for tomorrow." Liam listened as his site manager responded. "Great. See you then, Brock."

He set the phone down and swiveled in his chair. Damn, he needed a coffee. He'd had an early start, and he'd kill for a caramel macchiato. Zane and Mav gave him hell for liking sweet coffees, but he didn't care.

He looked out the window at the magnificent view of Manhattan. His gaze tracked across the skyline and found his friend Zane's building. He smiled. He picked up the phone again, and dialed.

"Zane Roth's office," a male voice said.

"Justin, it's Liam."

"One moment, Mr. Kensington."

A moment later a deep voice came on the line. "Zane Roth."

"You're actually at work. You managed to pull yourself away from the lovely Ms. O'Connor."

"Screw you, Kensington." But Zane's tone was happy, with a touch of smug.

"How are the legs?"

Zane made a sound. "Fine."

"How about dinner tonight?" he asked. "I'll call Mav, too. See if I can pry him out of his lab." The tech billionaire preferred inventing stuff to business meetings or parties.

"I'll check with Monroe," Zane said. "Sounds good. You cooking?"

"I think I will."

"Excellent. The one thing I don't argue about is your skill in the kitchen, Liam."

"Bring a bottle of something expensive."

Zane snorted. "Hell, no. I'll be raiding your cellar." Zane paused. "You okay?"

Liam frowned. "Why wouldn't I be?"

"I heard your father was in town."

Liam scowled. That explained why he had several messages from his father that he had no plans to return. "I don't give a flying fuck about him."

"I know, but I also know that families are complicated."

Liam released a breath. Zane's father had abandoned him and his mother when Zane was a kid.

Hell, Liam wished that Rupert Kensington had abandoned him.

"Well, I'm going to do my best to stay uncomplicated and avoid him."

"Good luck. See you tonight."

A moment later, Liam's assistant appeared in the doorway. Eleanor Rollings was a forty-year-old mother of two and the wife of a successful surgeon. She was attractive, had glossy, dark-brown skin and black hair she wore in all different styles. Today it was straightened and she wore it tied back in a ponytail. She was frighteningly competent.

"Your father's on the line," she said.

Liam ground his teeth together.

"I told him no," Eleanor said. "But the man is persistent."

"That's one word to describe him."

"You have a marketing meeting in fifteen minutes for the Borden Project."

His newest baby. "Thanks. I'll talk to him. It might make him stop calling."

Eleanor raised a brow, then closed the door behind her.

Liam snatched up the phone. "Father."

"Liam, my boy." His father's posh British accent came down the line. His tone was jovial.

"I'm busy. What do you want?"

"I'm in New York."

Liam waited.

His father's tone turned less jovial. "I want to see my son."

Sure. He wanted a loan, or for Liam to consider a deal, or for Liam to introduce him to somebody. "I'm busy."

31

"I'm also getting married. I want you to meet Cressida, and to invite you to the wedding."

Fuck. Liam felt a headache coming on. He really needed that coffee. He also wanted to throw something. "Father, I have a meeting now. I'm sorry, but I don't have the time to meet your future fourth wife."

"Liam—" An angry growl.

Liam hung up. Bloody hell, this would rile his mother up. And break the heart of Annabelle. Rupert's third wife actually loved him.

Liam wished his father would actually be a father to his youngest children. Annabelle had a boy and a girl, and Liam kept in touch. Did what he could to be a male role model in George and Amelia's lives.

Right. Meeting. He rose and fastened his suit jacket.

He strode out to see a slim brunette facing off with Eleanor.

"I *really* need a minute of Mr. Kensington's time," the woman said.

"Leave the paperwork on the desk," Eleanor said, tone unyielding.

The brunette wore a sleeveless purple dress, with a low-cut neckline. She spotted him, and her face lit up, her over-full lips forming a perfect pout.

"Mr. Kensington," she said in a breathy voice that would do Marilyn Monroe proud.

She looked vaguely familiar. Maybe from the Sales department? Or Finance?

"Leave it with Eleanor," he said. "I have a meeting."

The brunette sidestepped in front of him. "I can bring it back later."

Shit, she'd be lucky to be twenty-two.

"Leave it with Eleanor," he repeated.

She touched her hand to his chest. "I'm really good, Mr. Kensington...at my job. If there's *anything* I can do for you..."

An amused snort cut through the moment.

His head shot up.

He saw the blonde—medium-height, athletic body with curves in the right places packed into a long, gray skirt. Her blonde hair was loose around a bold face. She had strong features, intriguing, with a dimple in her chin. Her bright-green eyes were dancing with unhidden amusement.

Penn Channing.

His gut tightened. Luckily—or not, perhaps—he'd been so busy with work, he'd managed to stop himself from dropping by the Marketing floor for no good reason, just to get another glimpse of her.

"Why don't I stop by later with the file?" Ms. Breathy purred.

Liam dragged his gaze off Penn. "No, I—"

The woman leaned into him. "I don't mind, I can—"

"Yes, yes, Marilyn. We all know what you can do. How about you unhook your claws and run along?"

Ms. Breathy blinked, then glared at Penn.

Liam took the file the woman was holding and slapped it on Eleanor's desk. "You can go."

His tone finally got through, and her pouty lips pouted even more. She swiveled and stalked off.

"Close call." Penn held a file and a takeout coffee

cup. "Another second, and I'm pretty sure she would have shed that dress and asked to have your babies."

"Good morning," Liam said.

"I'm Penn Channing, from Marketing. I'm new."

"I remember you from the Nightingale House event, Ms. Channing."

She smiled. "I really do have a contract for you to sign." She held up the file. "For the Taunton budget."

"Leave it on the desk," he said.

Penn's smile widened, and against his will, his gaze dropped to her lips. Normal ones, no filler in sight, and perfectly shaped. He felt a pulse in his gut.

He frowned. He'd seen far more beautiful women than Penn from Marketing, but something about her—the intelligence in her eyes, the confidence she exuded—was intriguing.

She also didn't look like she was calculating his bank balance.

"The thing is, Lisa needs it signed now, and then I have a meeting to get to." Her lips twitched. "I come bearing bribes, although it seems kind of boring now, compared to Marilyn's offer."

He raised a brow.

She held out a coffee cup. "Caramel macchiato."

Shit. "Deal, hand over the coffee." He took the file, opened it. He'd already been over the Taunton budget at home last night after he'd had a drink with Zane, Monroe, and Mav.

He scrawled his name, then handed the file back to her and took the cup. Her fingers brushed his and Liam felt a tingle. He saw Penn frown.

"This is much better than Marilyn's offer," he said.

"Her name is Roberta," Eleanor said dryly. "She works in Purchasing."

Well, he'd been wrong on all counts.

Penn took the file. "Thanks." Without a pause, she turned on her heel.

Strangely, Liam didn't want to let her leave.

"Wait, is your meeting on the Borden Project?"

She glanced back over her shoulder. "Yes."

"I'm heading there, too. We can walk together."

For the first time in a long time, a woman didn't look thrilled to spend time with him.

Damned if Liam didn't like it.

Aspen

Walking down the hall, I was highly conscious of Liam Kensington behind me.

He was even more gorgeous up close and personal, wearing his custom-tailored blue suit, gray shirt, and blue tie. The tie made the bright blue of his eyes stand out, and his golden hair gleam. But it was the strong line of his jaw where my gaze lingered, and the sharp angle of his cheekbone. He'd been cleanshaven at the Nightingale House fundraiser a few days ago, but he had stubble today. I swallowed. I liked it.

Then I noted he was looking down, and my belly clenched. *Wait, was he looking at my ass?*

Then his gaze flicked up and met mine.

I felt the jolt. He emanated a sense of power and authority, with a dash of arrogance. Damn, the man packed a one-two punch.

A deep *woof* echoed down the corridor. I saw Liam frown. I heard another *woof*. *What in the world?*

We swiveled and I spotted a giant Saint Bernard bounding toward us.

I froze. I wasn't exactly a dog person. I'd been bitten by one doing surveillance on a cheating husband once. This one was big.

Really big.

And moving at full speed, a leash trailing behind it.

Liam shoved his coffee at me. I grabbed it, just as he stepped in front of me.

The dog did an expert dodge around Liam and jumped. Its paws hit me in the chest and I sucked in a shocked breath. I fell backward.

Strong arms caught me and my arms flailed. The dog jumped down.

My file went flying one way, and the coffee cup slammed into Liam's chest. Its lid flew off, and coffee spilled all over the fine gray fabric of his shirt.

Shit. It had to be hot. Without thinking, I pivoted, snatched a water bottle off a desk nearby and then tossed the water on him.

It caught his face and soaked his shirt.

He blinked, water dripping down his cheeks.

Oh. *God.* I'd just thrown coffee *and* water on a billionaire.

He arched an eyebrow. "I wasn't wet enough?"

"I was worried the coffee would scald you!"

The dog, clearly still excited, circled us, barking.

The leash had become tangled around our legs, and I felt it go taut. "Watch out—"

"Shit," Liam barked out.

He fell backward and I pitched forward.

He landed on his back and I landed smack on top of him. My mouth hit his, and our teeth clicked together.

I wasn't sure if I was embarrassed, horrified, or some other emotion that should make me want to crawl into bed and never come out.

The scent of coffee was strong, but under it, I picked up a masculine cologne—the woody smell of sandalwood. I had a sandalwood candle and it was my favorite.

He cupped the back of my head. "Are you all right?"

"Actually, you make a pretty good place to land." I winced. "Crap, that might have come out wrong."

He smiled.

I was up close and personal with that sexy smile. My lips just inches from his. His hard body stretched out under mine.

Then a furry head stuck itself in our faces and started licking.

Ew. I tried to push up and heard Liam grunt.

"Watch that knee."

Shit. I tried to fend off the very-happy-to-see-us-dog, and not emasculate Liam Kensington at the same time, and felt something well up in my chest.

"Don't you dare." Liam brought us both up to sitting. I was practically in his lap.

Laughter burst out of me. I was laughing so hard, my chest hurt.

Liam shook his head, but he was smiling. He gripped the dog's collar. "You, sit."

The dog sat its huge butt down, tongue lolling in a size-large, doggy grin.

"I...you..." I couldn't control my laugher. "Mr. Kensington—"

"Since we've been horizontal together, and kissed, you should call me Liam. And I'll call you Penn."

My laughter broke off. "We didn't kiss."

"Lips touched. That's a kiss."

"It is not!" The very last thing I needed to be thinking about was kissing Liam Kensington, in the middle of a damn undercover investigation.

A male assistant appeared, racing down the corridor. When he saw us, he skidded to a halt, horror reflected in his wide eyes. He looked at the dog, at us on the floor, at Liam's wet, coffee-stained shirt.

"Sir, I am so, *so* sorry. Mrs. Newhouse is here for an investment meeting, and she insisted on bringing that monster...I mean, dog, with her."

"It's fine, Richard. No harm done, except for my shirt."

The assistant grabbed the dog's lead and yanked the giant canine away, still mumbling apologies.

In a lithe move, Liam rose to his feet and held out a hand to me.

I took his hand, and felt a funny tingle up my arm. I barely resisted snatching my hand away.

Then, he towed me down the hall.

"What are you doing?" I tried to tug my hand free. "My file—"

He snatched the file up on the way past. "I need to change my shirt. I keep a spare in my office. Your hair is loose, and you're untucked. You can freshen up in my bathroom."

The man had a hard grip and kept ahold of me. We sailed past a startled Eleanor, and into his office.

I blinked. How did the man get any work done in here? It looked like the entire city was stretched out below us. I'd spend all day staring at the view.

The floors were dark wood, and his modern, metal-and-wood desk was front and center. Off to one side lay a circular, gray rug, with a sleek, futuristic couch and chairs on it.

"Bathroom's through there." He pointed to a doorway, then dropped my file on his desk and started shrugging out of his suit jacket.

I ducked in, noting the glossy marble and large mirror. There was a shower larger than mine at home. I quickly redid my hair and tucked my shirt back into my skirt.

"Thanks, I—"

When I stepped out of the bathroom, I was confronted by a shirtless Liam Kensington.

Oh. *Wow*. My mouth went dry.

His suit pants sat low on lean hips, and my gaze ran across his bare chest. I saw golden skin stretched over a lightly muscled chest and ridged abdomen.

What billionaire stayed in this kind of shape? He was working all the time, so I couldn't imagine how he could have all those delicious muscles.

He shrugged into a new shirt, and I watched the intriguing flex of his muscles.

Then I heard a low chuckle.

My head jerked up and I met amused blue eyes.

Oh, God. I'd been blatantly staring at him.

"Should I finish doing up the buttons, or do you need another minute?" he asked.

I felt the hot sting of embarrassment in my cheeks and turned. "Sorry, I..." Crap, what? I was too busy ogling you? "You must be used to people staring at you. You aren't exactly hard on the eyes."

Another amused chuckle.

"Come on," I said. "You were voted the most handsome billionaire bachelor. No need to be modest."

He stepped into view, shirt buttoned and tucked. "I don't have a lot of competition."

"Oh? I bet Zane Roth and Maverick Rivera would love to hear that."

Liam's lips twitched. "Those ugly cretins?"

I smiled back. Dammit, I didn't want to like the guy. I had to remember Erica and Jake. "Ah, in case you've forgotten, we have a meeting to get to."

"I hadn't forgotten. And now all the evidence of you tossing coffee and water over me is gone, we can go."

I grabbed my file off his desk, and we headed back down the corridor to the conference room. He reached past me and opened the door. As he passed by me, his cologne hit my senses. So yummy.

I fought back a shiver.

Shit. Get a hold of yourself, Aspen.

Or rather, I needed to get a hold of my hormones.

I didn't need an inconvenient attraction to Liam Kensington. One, every woman in Manhattan was attracted to the man. Two, I was working undercover at the Kensington Group, while negotiating with a white-collar-crime gang. Three, Jake's life was on the line. Things were complicated enough.

"Thank you," I murmured, then hightailed it around the glossy, black conference table to Abigail. "Signed." I handed her the file.

"Nice work." Her gaze flicked to Liam. "God, that man generates so many dirty fantasies."

I looked over. He stood at the head of the table, talking to his construction manager. He had one hand on a lean hip. Instantly, I pictured him shirtless in my head.

A flicker of heat ignited in my belly and I crossed my legs.

Stop thinking about the sexy billionaire. Think about the bad guys.

"Let's get started." Liam sat at the head of the conference table. His blue eyes met mine for a second, then he started talking.

Abigail leaned closer. "What was that?"

"What?"

"That look."

"What look? He looked at me for like, a millisecond."

Abigail frowned.

"Ms. Hosler, did you have something to share?" Liam asked.

He was looking at Abigail.

She cleared her throat. "No, sir."

I got busy taking notes. Everyone started talking about the Borden Project in the Bronx.

"Liam, we can decrease the size of the apartments and fit more in," one executive said. "It will increase profit significantly. We can also convert some space to more commercial offices—"

"No," Liam said. "This project isn't just about profit. It's about providing affordable, good quality homes, and rejuvenating the area. I don't need more profit."

There was a smattering of laughter around the table.

"I want a quality project. One that the Kensington Group can be proud of."

I stared at him. He wasn't what I expected at all.

"Now, on to the Ridge Project in Brooklyn."

Images of a partly constructed skyscraper appeared on the screen on the wall.

"The problems with the electrical have been sorted." One of the project managers leaned forward. "Work is progressing well."

I scribbled some more notes. I wasn't a huge fan of paperwork. I liked being in the field more.

"I want to see it," Liam said. "I've already talked to Brock about a site visit tomorrow. And it's time for marketing to start putting together the early preview plans."

The head of my area, Lisa, nodded. She was a tiny, intimidating woman of about sixty, with a perfect, ash-blonde bob haircut. "I can do a visit tomorrow. Abigail can come and take notes."

"Oh, I'm out of the office tomorrow," Abigail said.

"I'm sure Penn can fill in," Liam said.

My head shot up as he said my alias. He was looking at me, and everyone else turned to do the same.

"I'm sure Ms. Channing will be happy to attend," Lisa said.

"Sure thing." My burner phone buzzed. As the conversation moved on, I pulled it into my lap.

"Penn?" Abigail murmured. "He calls you by your first name? What exactly did you do to get him to sign that file?"

"Gave him a coffee. That's it." I decided not to mention knocking it all over him or seeing his bare chest. I looked at my phone in my lap and my pulse quickened.

There was a text from Nexus.

Meet in the coffee shop downstairs. 15 minutes.

As the meeting wound up, I breathed slowly and stayed relaxed. I didn't have long to get downstairs.

As everyone started to rise, I collected my things.

"Penn?"

I turned and braced, but Liam still made every cell in my body sit up and take notice. "Yes?"

"I hope you're okay with the site visit tomorrow."

"Absolutely."

"Great. Come by my office in the morning and we'll drive over together."

"Um, I can go with Lisa."

"She lives in Brooklyn, so she'll meet us there."

Darn. "Sure. All right."

"We're going early. Seven AM."

"Not a problem."

His smile made that lean, aristocratic face even more gorgeous. "See you tomorrow."

I hurried to the elevator, power walked across the lobby, then raced to the Busy Bean.

I pulled out my phone and tapped in a message.

I'm here.

People were coming and going from the coffee shop, and the baristas looked run off their feet. No one looked like a criminal mastermind.

They never did.

Some of the people I'd seen break the law were just greedy or desperate people who'd made bad choices. But others had normal faces hiding rotten hearts.

A woman with dyed black hair stopped beside me. Her eyes were blue, but they looked blank, cold.

"Be ready. You'll receive an envelope in the next few days. For now, leave this for the target to find."

She handed me a small note, then the woman was gone.

I dragged in a breath and headed back to the office.

Once I was inside the elevator, I opened the note.

Secrets never stay in the shadows.

My gut cramped. What trouble was Liam Kensington in?

4

SECRETS NEVER STAY IN THE SHADOWS

Liam

L iam dodged the hit, ducked his attacker's arm, and landed his own hard punch to the man's side.

His attacker grunted and staggered.

"Jesus, Kensington, what's with you today?" Mav grunted.

"He's kicking your ass, Mav," Zane called out across the indoor gym.

"He wants it more," another deep voice, one lined with grit, said.

Straightening, Liam glanced at Zane and their trainer, Simeon. The older man was lean, a little mean, and had no qualms about putting the three of them through their paces.

He taught them Krav Maga, and regularly kicked all their asses. He claimed he'd been in the Israeli military, but Zane swore he was an ex-Mossad spy.

Mav grabbed his water bottle from the corner of the

mats and chugged. Liam nabbed his towel and wiped his face.

"He seemed off last night at dinner, too." Mav scowled.

"Dinner was excellent, though," Zane said. "Monroe likes to bake, but she isn't fond of cooking. She loved your Beef Wellington, Liam."

Surprisingly, Monroe was fitting into their trio easily.

Zane was lucky. He'd found a woman who was down-to-earth, gorgeous, smart, and fun. And most importantly real.

"My father is getting married again," Liam said.

"Hell," Mav grunted.

Liam shrugged. "I looked up my new stepmother-to-be. She's twenty-five."

"God." Zane shook his head. "Sorry, Liam."

"But no doubt my father is in New York for more than just introducing his fiancée to his son," Liam said.

"Money," Mav grumbled, his voice holding an edge.

"My father will leave New York eventually." Liam wiped the back of his neck. "He always does. And I'll wait to see both his wedding and divorce in the society pages."

Zane gripped Liam's shoulder and squeezed.

"Let's get together Friday night," Mav said. "I got my hands on a bottle of thirty-seven-year-old Lagavulin, and it has our names on it."

"Sounds great." Liam glanced at his Patek Philippe. "Shit, I need to shower and get to the office. I have an early off-site meeting." He smiled, thinking of tangling with Penn again. Without the Saint Bernard involved, this time.

"What's that smile?" Zane studied him like he was a hot, billion-dollar deal.

"What smile?" Liam grabbed his workout bag. "Thanks, Simeon."

The older man grunted. "That smile says woman."

"I have a site visit," Liam said.

"Woman," Simeon insisted.

Liam waved and disappeared into the locker room before he got interrogated.

He was highly conscious of the fact that Penn was an employee, which made her off-limits. He'd watched his father sleep through half of his own company, and it was a line Liam didn't cross.

No matter how intriguing he found the lovely, confident Penn.

He showered and dressed in his bespoke Henry Poole suit, and drove his Aston Martin DB11 to the office. He parked in the garage and took the executive elevator to his office.

He loved being in the office early or late at night—when it was quiet, no one else was around.

He scanned the tiles and glass, the vase of fresh flowers on the reception desk. His name etched on the wall.

Kensington Group was *his*. He'd built it from the ground up. He was the one who'd taken the risks, worked endless all-nighters, and bled for it. No doubt he'd been privileged—one thing his father had given him was a good education, but after college, Rupert had tried to bring Liam to heel.

Liam had actually wanted to join the British Army. Rupert had wanted him to take over the family business in London. And run everything his father's way. Rupert was fond of handshake deals and business that didn't sit well with Liam.

Thanks to his father's interference—he'd been buddies with a few generals—the Army wasn't an option. He'd decided to start his own company from the ground up in order to stick it to his father.

Liam was bloody proud of everything he'd forged on his own—every brick, beam, and wall.

He sat behind his desk and sorted through some messages that Eleanor had left for him.

"Hello, there," a throaty, female voice drawled.

Liam looked up, frowned.

A tall woman leaned in his doorway. She wore a long, fur coat, and had a cloud of styled black hair, and wide, almond-shaped eyes.

It took him a second to place her. To be fair, he'd only met her once in person, and he was used to seeing her in her underwear plastered on billboards.

Geneva Sorensen.

She was the model of the moment—taking New York by storm. She'd worn some infamous dress to the Met Gala, and was headlining Fashion Week.

They'd met at a party a few weeks back, and she'd put both her phone number and her hotel key card in his pocket.

He hadn't been tempted to use either. A few months

ago, she'd been seen partying with his father on a yacht in the South of France.

"Geneva."

"Liam." She tossed her head back in a move that had to be practiced. "You never called."

"How did you get up here?"

"The guard downstairs recognized me." Her perfect lips formed a smile. "I told him we were *special* friends."

Liam made a note to talk to the head of security. "Well, I'm afraid I'm on my way out—"

She strode in, and her coat shifted, giving him a view of her long, leggy body clad only in bronze lingerie.

Ah, hell. She was gorgeous, of course, and he supposed he should be worried that he barely felt more than a blip of interest.

"Geneva, this is my place of business. I've a full day ahead—"

"We can have so much fun together." Her voice was a sexy purr. "Cancel your meetings."

Liam sighed. *Seriously?*

There was movement in the doorway and Penn appeared. Today, she was wearing wide-legged black pants, and a red top with a tie at the neck. Her pale-blonde hair was up in a bun.

She eyed Geneva and her lips twitched. She looked like she was trying not to laugh.

"Good morning, Mr. Kensington," Penn said.

Geneva pulled her coat closed, turned and stuck out a hip. It was a pose he'd seen her use on the catwalk.

"Go away." Geneva waved a hand at Penn.

Penn raised a brow. "Sorry, I work for him, not you."

Liam rose. "Do not move, Penn."

"You'd prefer to spend time with *this*." Geneva waved a hand at Penn again.

Penn gave a mock wince and slapped a hand to her chest. "Oh no, my self-esteem is shattered." The sarcasm came through loud and thick.

The model made an annoyed sound.

"Look, lady," Penn said. "Like I said, I work for him, and we have a meeting. You really want to be gone before Eleanor arrives, because she'll eviscerate you."

Geneva sniffed and her gaze met Liam's. "You're turning me down?"

Liam put his hands in his pockets. "It's why I didn't call."

He saw a flicker of disappointment followed by a dose of embarrassment, and it made him realize how young she was.

"You're a beautiful woman, Geneva—"

"Right." Then, she tossed her hair back. "You won't get another chance." She strode out, almost running over Penn in the process.

Penn watched the woman go. "Do you think she practices that head toss in the mirror?" Penn shook her head. "So, your morning is off to a good start."

He growled. "Shut it. Let's go." He paused. "Did you bring coffee?"

She turned to Eleanor's desk and grabbed two takeout cups that she must have rested there. She handed him one.

"For the record, I would prefer to spend time with you," he said.

Their gazes met. He saw something move through her green eyes.

His gut tightened. *Shit*. She was an employee. "Penn—"

When he used her name, a strange look twisted her features, then her face went blank. "We'd better go. The car's waiting."

He sucked in a breath. "Let me get my coat."

Liam turned and grabbed his overcoat off the back of one of the guest chairs. That's when he spied a folded piece of paper on the chair.

Frowning, he picked it up. *Where had this come from?* He opened it.

Secrets never stay in the shadows.

He felt a chill run down his spine. *What the hell?*

He had no idea what it meant or where the hell it had come from. Had Geneva left it? Was it a threat?

He saw Penn watching him.

"Everything okay?" she asked.

Nodding, he balled the note and tossed it on his desk. "Let's go."

Aspen

I sat in the back of the town car, Liam beside me. He was on his phone, and already had responded to several messages.

Another assistant sat in the car, too. A young, well-dressed man with a large camera.

Liam finished his call and sat back in his seat. "So, we'll meet the construction manager, Brock, and Lisa at the building. We're going to take a tour of the upper levels. Manny, here, will take some photos for the early preview marketing."

Manny held up his camera.

"Penn, you take notes on everything."

I nodded. "Got it."

I eyed Liam. He seemed to have forgotten the confrontation with the supermodel of the long legs, pouty lips, not many clothes. I shifted in my seat. Did women throw themselves at him all day long? The man could have his pick.

My belly turned over. I really didn't like that idea.

The car slowed to a stop, and Liam climbed out. He held a hand out to me.

I took it and instantly I felt a tingle up my arm. *Crap.* I did not need this. I let go quickly.

I looked up at the building that was still under construction. A crane was perched high in the air, and there was temporary fencing around the base. There was also scaffolding everywhere, covered in workers in brightly colored workwear.

"Liam." A bearded man strode out of the building. He wore khaki work pants, heavy boots, and a yellow jacket over a chambray work shirt.

"Brock. Tell me you're on schedule and under budget."

The site manager grinned. "Mostly."

Lisa appeared, her heels clicking as she strode down the pavement.

Liam introduced them all.

"Okay," Brock said. "Follow my commands, stay close, and keep behind all barriers. We're heading up to the 65th floor and it's still under construction."

A small wave of queasiness hit me. I wasn't afraid of heights exactly. I just didn't love them.

Brock led us through the fence and we passed some workers carrying giant tools. Manny walked gingerly, like he might get dirty. I thought Liam would look out of place in his clearly expensive dark suit, but he didn't. He was asking Brock detailed questions.

We stopped in front of a metal construction lift attached to the side of the building. My throat tightened, like someone was choking me.

Oh, no. No. No. No.

It was made of sturdy metal, and I'm sure it was up to code, but to me, it looked temporary and rickety.

I backed up a step.

Lisa and Manny stepped into the metal cage, chatting with Brock.

Pull yourself together, Chandler. You're a damn private investigator.

"Penn?"

I swiveled my head and found Liam watching me with all-too-perceptive eyes. I had to admit that I hated him using my fake name. The twins called me Penn sometimes, but at the moment, it was just a reminder that I was lying.

"It's just that...elevators are supposed to be on the *inside* of the building." Protected by layers of concrete.

He cocked his head. "I assure you that it's safe."

Shit. My brain didn't care about facts. Straightening my spine, I marched in and stood behind Lisa.

Brock clanged the door closed.

"Won't take too long." The man touched the controls.

With a jerk, the lift started up.

My pulse accelerated. I felt like concrete was filling my chest.

The damn walls of the lift were made of mesh, and I could see out. *Ugh.* A hot flush washed over me. *Hold it together.*

A body shifted closer to mine and Liam's cologne hit me. The man smelled like sin. I'd be lying if I said I hadn't burned my sandalwood candle last night, while lying naked in my bed, and perhaps thinking naughty things about Liam Kensington.

"Okay?" he whispered.

"Peachy."

His fingers brushed mine, hidden from the others by his jacket.

Desperate, I latched on. "I'm...not fond of heights."

"I can tell."

"Or small metal cages temporarily attached to buildings."

His beautiful lips quirked. "I guess it's my turn to save you. Just look at me."

I snorted. "You're far too easy to look at, Mr. Kensington."

"I told you to call me Liam. Especially since we're holding hands."

I didn't think that was a good idea. I should let his hand go, but I couldn't. I stared into clear blue eyes.

"I hate showing any weakness," I whispered.

"I know the feeling."

I had to look away. I glanced to the side and saw the city far, far below.

Nausea hit me. "Oh, God."

"Penn, look at me."

I turned back to him. "We're *really* high up."

"We're high up at the office."

"With perfectly safe panes of glass between us and the killer drop."

His fingers squeezed mine. "I've got you."

My stomach flip-flopped. For a second, I wondered what it would feel like if Liam Kensington *really* had me.

Oh, no. I cleared my throat. I had to get this under control. I'd learned long ago to be self-sufficient. My father's betrayal and mom's breakdown meant I'd had to step up. I'd had to help my mom and sisters. I'd learned to rely on no one but myself.

Everyone else invariably let you down.

The cage jerked to a halt and I gasped.

"Here we are." Brock opened the door.

Liam gave my fingers another squeeze and then let go.

"Thanks." I whispered.

"My pleasure."

The low, sexy drawl made my brain descend into the gutter. My brain wanted to roll around in all the ways Liam Kensington could murmur "my pleasure" to me, preferably while naked, with his hands on other parts of my body.

Jeez. I strode off the lift.

A stiff breeze whipped through the half-built level.

On one side were just concrete support pillars, and the open edge was very visible.

I stifled a whimper. That part was cordoned off by a metal barrier. Perfectly safe.

"Liam, here's the wiring I mentioned to you." Brock led Liam to the more constructed part of the level. Manny started snapping pictures.

"Okay." Lisa turned, hands on her hips. "Look at these views."

I'd had enough views for today. I pulled out my tablet. As Lisa called out ideas for the marketing plans and details she wanted to highlight, I wrote them all down.

My mind wandered. Doyle and Nexus were ready to strike. I'd left that damn note for Liam. I could feel the threat growing like a thundercloud. I wanted this done so I could get Jake home to Erica.

I glanced at Liam and my belly did a slow turn. His suit accented his lean, fit body and I blew out a breath. I liked him. I'd expected an arrogant asshole, and while I didn't doubt he could be arrogant, he seemed genuine.

What did Nexus have on him?

Manny's camera clicked. "What's this large glass area?"

I glanced down and saw the sloped glass that speared off from this level to the one down below.

Brock turned. "That's the vaulted roof of the club level below."

I studied the sharply sloped glass and shuddered.

Manny leaned out against the metal railing, snapping more pictures.

Suddenly, there was a screech of metal.

"Fuck!" Manny cried.

The railing gave way.

Manny fell, his camera hitting his chest, then he slapped down on his belly against the sloped glass.

Oh, shit.

Lisa screamed.

Manny started sliding and I realized he'd slide all the way to the edge and off the side of the building.

I didn't think, I acted.

I leaped after the young man, trying to grab him.

5

BLACKMAIL

Liam

*F*ucking hell.

Liam watched Penn dive toward the flailing Manny.

She hit the concrete, then slid onto the glass. She managed to snap one hand around Manny's wrist. Her other arm flew out and she grabbed a bar of the metal railing.

Fuck. Liam lunged toward them with Brock beside him. The construction manager was cursing steadily.

Liam saw a pale-faced Lisa out of the corner his eye. "Stay back," he barked.

He dropped to his knees beside Penn and grabbed her arm.

"Don't move." *Hell.* One wrong move and Manny would pull her over.

"Not...planning to," she said through gritted teeth. The strain was clear on her face.

"Brock!" Liam yelled.

"On it." The big man went flat on his front and reached down, trying to grab Manny.

The young photographer flailed. "*Please*. Please don't let go!"

"I won't," Penn said. "Quit moving."

"Manny, hold still," Liam growled.

He tightened his grip on Penn. Damn, the panicked idiot was going to pull her over.

"Got him." Brock twisted a hand in the back of Manny's shirt and started pulling him up.

As Manny scrambled over the edge, Penn slid backward.

She was still holding Manny.

"You can let go now," Liam said.

She blew out a breath, then released the young man. Then she glanced over the edge, and all the color drained from her face.

"Here." Liam wrapped an arm around her.

She burrowed into him, clinging tight. "God."

"You're afraid of heights, but you dove after Manny like a superhero."

"I couldn't let him fall. I just reacted."

Yes, but she'd done the opposite of what he suspected most people would do.

She'd risked her own life.

Liam's pulse was still pounding crazily. He pulled her closer, practically into his lap. He leaned back against the concrete support pole.

His suit was covered in dust, and her hair had fallen

loose and was spilling around her shoulders. He stroked a hand over it. *Shit.*

Her hands twisted in his shirt. She pulled in a shaky breath.

"Sorry," she muttered.

"Don't be."

"I'll get a grip on it soon." She dragged in a shuddering breath. He saw that she was calming herself. Most people would be a panicked mess.

Nearby, Manny was hyperventilating. Brock shoved the man's head between his legs while Lisa patted his back.

"I want off this building," Manny said. "I want my feet on the ground."

"Okay, just breathe," Brock said.

Liam turned his attention back to Penn when he noticed a smear of red on the concrete beside him.

He frowned. Manny appeared fine. Then he looked down and saw Penn looking at him.

"It's okay," she said, "I just scraped my hands."

He grabbed her palms. She'd scraped them badly when she leaped after Manny. There were bits of grit embedded in her skin.

"These need to be cleaned. Now."

"It's fine, I'll—"

"No. Brock, you have a first aid kit?"

"In the lift."

"I'll get it." Liam shifted, and felt her hands tighten on him. Then he watched her steel herself and let him go.

Damn, there was a deep core of strength in this woman.

He found the red plastic box emblazoned with a white cross on it in the lift. As he was heading back, Brock and Lisa were standing on either side of a still-shaking Manny.

"We'll get him down," Brock said.

Liam nodded. "I'll clean Penn's hands, then we'll get the lift once it comes back."

"She saved his life," Brock rumbled. "I hadn't even processed what was happening, and she'd already moved."

Liam frowned.

"Penn?" Manny's voice wobbled. "Thank you."

She nodded, leaning back against the pole. "Sure thing. Glad you're okay."

Brock met Liam's gaze. "I need to report this to health and safety."

"Do it. And have all the railings checked. And do a refresher for all employees about not leaning out on the railings."

Manny held up a hand. "Lesson learned. Trust me."

Once the lift was gone, Liam crouched beside Penn. Her eyes were closed.

"How are you doing?" he asked.

"Great. With my eyes closed, I can pretend I'm back on the ground."

He opened the kit. "I can't believe what you did, especially when you're afraid of heights."

"Not afraid, per se. Let's go with not fond of."

He fought a smile and pulled out some gauze and antiseptic.

"And I just did the right thing," she said.

Liam held up her palm. She had strong, competent fingers. Her nails were short and painted with a clear gloss.

"No, I see daily that a lot of people don't do the right thing."

Green eyes met his. "You might be hanging out with the wrong people."

"Undoubtedly."

He wiped antiseptic over her scrapes and she hissed.

"Sorry."

"Distract me," she said.

"Are you single?" Shit, that was *not* what he meant to say. "I mean, is there anyone I should call?"

She eyed him. "No."

"Family?"

"My mom lives upstate, and my sisters live with me. They're at college. You'd be doing me a favor not to call them."

"Ah, you don't get on?"

"Oh, no, it isn't that. They'd panic. And my sisters are drama queens."

"What about your father?"

She shrugged. "Out west. He moves a lot. He calls occasionally."

"So, your parents are divorced?"

"Yes. I was fourteen. They divorced, with a whole mess of shouting and bitterness."

"I'm sure mine could beat that," Liam said.

Penn winced, and not from his ministrations. "Sorry. I...know a little of your family history."

Most of the world did. "It's complicated."

"All families are." She shrugged. "We just keep on, focus on the good bits when we can, and deal with the messy bits."

He took a moment, staring at her. "You're one-of-a-kind, Penn."

"Thank you, Mr. Kensington."

"What's it going to take to get you to call me Liam? We've kissed—"

"We did not."

"Held hands."

She rolled her eyes.

"And now I'm acting as your personal nurse."

He was so close to her, and he saw something move through her gaze. She looked conflicted.

Hell, maybe this attraction was one sided? He really didn't like the thought of that.

"Liam." She cleared her throat. "We should go."

"Yes." He finished pressing on the bandage. "Try not to be a hero again today. Let these hands heal."

She gave him a faint smile. "We'll see."

He couldn't stop himself cupping her cheek.

He heard her swift intake of breath and the air between them charged.

"I find you very intriguing," he murmured. "The sharp wit, the smart mind, the courageous heart. The curvy body."

"I'm sure a pair of long legs and a stunning face will intrigue you tomorrow," she said, her voice husky.

Liam wasn't so sure. He stroked her cheek and saw heat flicker in her eyes.

"This is a bad idea," she said.

"No doubt. I don't get involved with employees."

"That's a good rule." Her gaze dropped to his lips.

With a groan, Liam leaned forward and kissed her.

For a second, she froze, then she moaned and gripped his head. Her mouth opened under his.

The kiss went from slow and hot to fast and molten in a flash. *Shit.* Pure desire hit him like a fist. Her tongue stroked his, and her taste filled him.

He dragged her closer. He swallowed her next moan. *He needed more.*

He heard the clank of the lift arriving. They jerked apart, panting.

"Shit," she muttered, then scrambled up.

Hell. Liam looked at her bandaged hands. This wasn't the time, or the place.

"This...didn't happen," she said.

He frowned. "It sure as hell did."

She shook her head. "No, I..." A flash of sadness crossed her face. "I'm sorry."

He wondered what she was apologizing for, but before he could respond, she turned and strode into the elevator.

Liam frowned. This wasn't the time for this, but he did know that Penn tugged at him. Stirred something in him that he wanted to explore.

Not now, but he would make the time. *Soon.*

Aspen

A siren sounded in the distance.

I stood in the dirty, smelly alley a block from the Kensington Group building, and wished I was in a hundred other places.

After the morning's events, the rest of the day had been blissfully uneventful.

I hadn't seen Liam.

Okay, I'd actively avoided seeing him.

I'd kissed a person of interest to my investigation. I'd allowed myself to get distracted.

I swallowed a groan. *Idiot.*

It had been the best kiss of my life. I blew out a breath. Just my luck.

The last guy I'd dated had been a DEA agent. I thought he liked the fact that I was dedicated to my job, but turned out he wanted a sweet, uncomplicated woman who wouldn't work, but instead, would stay home, cook meals, and iron his shirts.

I'd told him to go back to the 1950s.

His kisses had never knocked me off kilter like Liam's had.

Shit. "You shouldn't be kissing billionaires, Aspen."

Even without everything going on, Liam Kensington was way out of my league. He'd grown up wealthy, and moved in the top echelons of New York society, and was really, really rich. I was none of those things.

Erica had called an hour ago for an update. I made myself think of her tear-stained face, and poor Jake locked up in a cell somewhere.

My friend had also shared some news. She'd just found out she was pregnant.

Damn. I felt tears burn the back of my eyes. Poor Erica was alone and scared, and what should be a fantastic, happy moment for her was terrifying.

It wouldn't matter soon.

It felt like battery acid settled in my gut. I'd gotten a text from Nexus.

The blackmail happened tonight.

I scanned the alley, waiting for my contact.

Then, Liam Kensington wouldn't want to kiss me anymore.

He'd hate me.

I tasted bile.

A noise echoed through the alley.

I stiffened, and a man appeared, partly hidden by the shadows.

"Hello, Ms. Channing."

He had a low voice, no accent that I could detect. He didn't come any closer, and was careful not to show his face.

My pulse jumped. I felt something lurch inside me. "Hello, Mr. Doyle."

The man inclined his head.

He was so close. *Take him down.*

I wrestled for some control. *Jake. Think of Jake.*

"Here." Doyle held out a large envelope, and I took it. "Give it to Kensington. Tonight. Tell him that I have a video, as well. No demands yet. I want him to stew for a bit."

I kept my breathing even. "Okay."

"He's working late. You'll find him in his office."

I nodded. "What's in—?"

I realized I was talking to myself. Doyle was gone.

I hustled out of the alley. I stopped under a streetlight and opened the envelope.

It was filled with glossy photos that caused my breath to catch. For a second, I thought it was Liam in the pictures, but then I realized the naked man on the bed was older.

Rupert Kensington.

There were four women in the bed as well, in various states of undress, doing various things to the man.

Ew.

In one shot, one woman was looking directly at the camera, with what she probably thought was a sultry look.

Nausea swelled through me. Not a woman, a girl.

I flicked through more pictures.

Fuck. They were all very young, and my guess, very underage.

I shoved the photos back in the envelope.

Nexus was going to blackmail Liam with shots of his father.

I dragged in a deep breath. Sometimes I hated my job. I pressed a palm to my eyes. A flicker in my temple warned me a headache was threatening.

Then I lifted my chin.

My job was to get Jake back to Erica. I didn't want to make Liam suffer, but the man had resources, Jake and Erica didn't.

And if I got lucky, I could uncover who Doyle was, and turn him over to the police. Bring Nexus down.

Unfortunately, Liam couldn't know that I was really Aspen Chandler, private investigator.

For a while longer, I had to be Penn Channing, blackmailer.

I dragged in a breath and headed down the sidewalk.

My personal phone pinged. I pulled it out and saw a message from Briar.

I'm making fried chicken tonight. You going to be late?

I tapped on the screen.

Shouldn't be late.

I doubted I'd feel much like eating, though.

OK. Juno's on a date, so just you and me.

Apparently, Juno was surviving her break up just fine. I slid my phone away. I had my sisters to go home to after this. I'd just hold onto that thought to get me through.

I pulled out my Kensington Group key card and held it to the scanner. The door slid open. In the lobby, I waved at the night guard.

I resisted the urge to fidget in the elevator.

The executive office level was mostly shadowed. There was no one in the cubicles, or glass-walled offices. I saw a light on at the end of the hall in Liam's large office.

I paused in the doorway.

At the big desk, he was bent over a file, his brow creased.

So handsome.

Now I had to cause him pain.

No, Nexus was causing him pain. I would do my best to stop them.

I stepped inside and Liam's head shot up.

His frown melted away to a smile.

"Penn. How are the hands?"

"Fine."

He must have picked up my vibe, because he sat back in his chair, his gaze locked on me. "What's wrong?"

Steeling myself, I strode to his desk and dropped the envelope on it.

"Secrets don't stay in the shadows," I said.

He reached for the envelope, his face hardening. "You going to tell me what's going on?"

"Open it."

I watched him pull the photos out. I saw disgust, followed by a rush of anger and a mix of other emotions before he reined them in. I only saw them because I was used to looking for the smallest expressions as part of my job. I kept my face blank.

"What is this?" he asked carefully.

"Exactly what it looks like. Blackmail."

A muscle ticked in his jaw. "You're blackmailing me with this filth? Fuck, I should've known you were a fake. Just another bloody user."

His words hit hard, but I kept the cool look on my face. "I represent a group of business people."

"Business people?" He made a sound. "Criminals. This—" he stabbed a finger at the envelope "—hurts more than just my poor excuse of a father. These girls, my mother, my stepmother, siblings. There are children involved."

I fought to stay unmoved.

"It doesn't have to," I said.

"The real Penn shows her face. Is Penn even your name?"

"You can protect your family."

He looked at the desk, his face twisting. "How much?"

"I'll let you know. Think on it." I swiveled and headed for the door. "By the way, I'll be staying in my job here in the office until this is done. You try and remove me, or you call the cops, the photos will hit the web."

"You played me well. I was just starting to think you might be different."

His words put pain in my chest and my legs wanted to stumble, but I stayed strong.

"Just another snake," he said. "Kudos, Penn, I didn't see you coming."

"I'll be in touch." I bit my lip hard, and didn't turn back.

"Go and slither under your rock. I won't let you get away with this."

I stayed silent, bleeding inside as I walked away.

6

ALL A LIE

Liam

L iam sat in the armchair, cradling a glass of Scotch. He took a long swig, his insides burning.

Fuck. He wanted to hit something. He took another long sip. He wasn't sure what glass he was on. The open bottle rested on the coffee table.

He barely saw the view of Madison Square Park, or the Flatiron Building.

His cell phone vibrated on the table and this time he glanced at it. It had rung a few times this evening. He saw his mother's name.

Great. He really didn't have time for his mother right now.

But Diane Kensington Cavendish Donahue wasn't one to give up easily. She'd keep calling and calling.

"Hello, Mother."

"Liam, darling. How's my son?"

Shitty. "Fine. And you? How's Florida?"

"Oh, I'm having a lovely visit with the Palermos."

"That's wonderful."

A pause. "Is everything all right? You sound off."

"Just a long day."

"Well, I have unpleasant news, Liam." She sniffed. "I heard from a friend back in London that your father is on the rocks with his latest *wife*." She said wife the same way someone would say rotten fish. "I can't believe that arrogant, selfish man. If he divorces again, it will be all over the papers, and it'll be tossed in my face."

Yes, because it was all about her. Liam loved his mother, and he knew she loved him in her own way, but it wasn't a warm, vibrant, solid thing. It was dependent on Liam giving her everything that she wanted and ensuring she lived the life she was used to. He supplemented the settlement she'd received from her divorce, and she always stayed with him when she came to New York, whether it was convenient for him or not.

If those photos got out, his mother would have an epic meltdown. And he'd have to pick up the pieces.

"We can't control what he does, Mother."

She sniffed again. "Isn't there something you can do?"

Liam rolled his eyes. *Sure, I can control who my father fucks or marries.* "No, there isn't. I don't want anything to do with him, and I suggest you just ignore him."

"You could at least try, Liam." His mother released a breath. "Sometimes you sound just like him. I've always worried you'd turn out just like that man."

Liam ground his teeth together. *Thanks, Mother.* "I really need to go now."

"Very well. We have pre-dinner drinks soon. Goodbye, Liam."

He tossed the phone on the coffee table and took a large sip of Scotch. He savored the burn. He just wanted to be left alone.

There was the bleep of a lock. His front door opened and he swallowed a growl.

Only two people had the code to enter.

"What the fuck, Kensington?" Mav prowled in like a panther, ready to strike.

Zane followed behind him, worry on his face. Both were dressed casually in jeans.

"You aren't answering your phone." Zane put his hands on his hips. "And you missed our rock-climbing session this evening." Zane's gaze dropped to the bottle on the coffee table. "Shit."

"I'm fine." Liam rose, and walked to arched, wood-framed windows. He stared blindly at the traffic on 5th Avenue below.

"Is it your father?" Mav asked.

Liam's gut felt like a rock. The pictures were singed into his eyeballs.

His fucking father.

"Yes and no."

Zane dropped onto the arm of the cream couch, watching him steadily. Zane was the king of Wall Street because he was so good at reading people.

"There's a woman," Zane said. "Simeon was right."

Liam sucked in a breath. He was trying not to think of that certain, traitorous blonde.

Penn, the promise of her, was all a lie. Their connection was a lie.

Liam drained his drink, then swiveled, pulled back his arm, and threw the glass.

The heavy crystal hit the wall, then fell to the wood floor and shattered.

"Ah, hell." Mav grabbed three more glasses from the built-in bar, then poured more Scotch. He took a glass and drank it all before handing the others to Liam and Zane.

"I've told you," Mav said. "You fuck them, and that's it." Mav poured himself more of the amber liquid.

"Quiet, Mav." Zane's gaze moved back to Liam. "Who is she?"

"She started work at Kensington Group recently." Liam ground his teeth together. "You remember the woman who stopped that guy hitting his ex-wife at the Nightingale House fundraiser?"

"The blonde in green?" Mav said.

"Yeah. She's smart, funny, has a sharp wit."

"And is easy on the eyes," Mav grumbled, staring into his glass.

"A curvy, fit blonde." Liam swirled his drink. "Strong face, not beautiful per se, but attractive."

"And?" Zane prompted.

Hell. Liam dropped back into a sleek, modern armchair. "I liked her. Didn't seem to care about my money. She was..."

"Real," Zane murmured.

Liam met his friend's gaze and saw that Zane understood. Zane had found that in Monroe.

"I didn't see it coming. She even dived after a guy who fell on our site visit today in Brooklyn. On the sixty-fifth floor. She risked her life to save him. But she's all a fucking lie."

His friends both frowned.

"She came to my office tonight."

Mav set his glass down. "I'm guessing this is where the story goes sideways."

"She instigated a play. Blackmail." Liam nodded to the envelope on the coffee table.

Mav reached for it.

"Don't. Unless you want to see fucked-up photos of my father with underage girls. Multiple girls, at the same time."

"Fuck." Mav sagged back.

"What does she want?" Zane asked.

Liam sighed. "I don't know. She hasn't made any demands yet."

"It'll be money." Mav swirled his Scotch. "It's always money."

"My fucking father. This will destroy Annabelle, the kids will get hit. They're so young." Innocent. "My mother will catch the edge, too, and have a meltdown. His new fiancée. Everyone will be dragged through the mud, and added to that, there are four girls who were too young to consent to this. They'll have their lives ripped apart." Liam scraped a hand over his face.

"How do you want to play this?" Zane asked.

"First, I need to see what they want."

"They?"

"Penn says she represents a group."

With a growl, Mav knocked back his second glass of Scotch.

"Call Vander," Zane said.

Vander Norcross was former military, turned owner of a security firm based in San Francisco. The man was good—scary good. He'd helped Zane and Monroe, and he did a lot of work for Roth Enterprises.

Liam had his own in-house security at Kensington Group, but they specialized in protecting buildings and construction sites, not blackmail.

"You need intel," Zane said. "Find out who the hell this Penn is, and more about this group."

Liam nodded. "I can't let those pictures get out. Not for my fucking father, but for my family, and for those girls. Even if they thought they were on board, they're children."

Mav and Zane nodded.

"I'll call Vander. And then all I can do is wait for the fucking shoe to drop. See what their demands are."

It didn't feel like a shoe. It felt like an axe.

Dammit, he really wanted to punch someone.

Zane gripped Liam's shoulder. "We've got your back. Whatever you need, whenever you need it."

Mav nodded.

Liam felt a punch of warmth cutting through the ice of betrayal filling him.

These two men had been there for him for years. He trusted them, and he knew he had their full support.

He barely knew Penn. Her betrayal shouldn't cut this much.

"Thanks, guys." He straightened. "Whatever happens, I'll deal. Protect my family, and find a way for my father to answer for his fucked-up choices."

His friends nodded.

"Then I'll bring Penn, or whatever her real name is, down."

Zane frowned. "I'm sorry, Liam. Sorry she played you. Sorry you liked her."

Grabbing the bottle, Liam poured another drink. "It doesn't matter."

But his gut was still a mass of thorny knots.

Zane tapped his fingers on the arm of his chair, his face thoughtful. "Seems strange that a blackmailer out for a big payday would almost dive off a building to save a stranger, though."

Liam stilled with the glass halfway to his mouth.

"Just another way to earn Liam's trust and deflect suspicion," Mav said. "Women are cunning."

That had to be it. Liam sipped, and decided he might just get drunk.

Aspen

I finished typing up some files and scanned the office floor.

I hadn't seen Liam today.

Probably a good thing. Pressing my palms flat to the

desk, I tried to find some calm. I knew I was doing my job, what needed to be done, but dammit, it wasn't easy knowing he hated my guts right now.

My hands stung, reminding me of my scrapes. Wincing, I eased up. I'd slathered them with antiseptic cream this morning and put some bandages on. They were already looking better.

Erica walked past my desk. She looked tired, and when she caught my eye, she gave me a small smile. I'd called her this morning to tell her things were heating up. That we were getting closer to bringing Jake home.

"Penn." Abigail appeared at my desk. "You're needed for an off-site gig at the Woolworth Building."

I rose. "Sure."

"Take notes, and keep the boss on track. I'm supposed to go, but I had a vaccination yesterday and I feel like death warmed over."

She looked pale and clammy. "Sorry, hope you feel better. So just Lisa going?"

"No, not Lisa, Mr. Kensington."

I froze. "Oh, well—"

"You're on first-name basis with him, and you're a hero after yesterday." Abigail winked.

I smiled weakly. "Okay."

"Five minutes. He'll meet you downstairs."

Great. I gathered my stuff. I had my Glock tucked safely inside my bag.

I took the elevator down. Light poured into the lobby and my heels clicked on the marble tiles. I saw Liam by the door. He wore a gray suit today that fit him well and my belly clenched. The sunlight glinted off his hair.

I straightened, just as he turned. His face hardened, his eyes turning icy.

And I felt it like a burn.

"Where's Abigail?" he demanded.

"She can't make it."

He looked away, his jaw working. "I don't have time to arrange for someone else. Let's go." He strode out to the sleek, black Aston Martin waiting at the curb.

He opened the passenger door for me and I slid into the sports car. God, the seats were buttery, black leather and it smelled expensive.

Liam circled the car and got in the driver's seat. The engine purred and we zoomed off.

The atmosphere in the car was Arctic.

This was not going to be a pleasant outing.

"How long have you been a criminal?" he clipped.

"Your father's the criminal."

"My father's a first-class asshole. I've always known that."

I heard the bitterness in his voice and I stayed silent.

"Tell me what you fucking want," Liam growled.

"When the time's right." I still hadn't heard from Doyle.

"I just want to know," Liam said. "The lives of my family are on the line. My step-siblings are young, innocent."

I crossed my legs. I had to remember Jake. Erica. Their child.

Liam growled. "You don't know what your group wants, do you?"

I stared ahead through the windshield.

"You're just a lackey, waiting for orders."

I dragged in a breath, hating the acid dripping from his voice. "Everything will happen when it needs to."

"You're a cold one. Got ice in those veins, Penn?"

He jerked the wheel and we flew down a side street. I pressed a hand to the door.

"Just another heartless, cunning bitch."

I closed my eyes.

"And a liar. I hate liars most of all. Most people are full of shit, but I'm usually good at spotting them."

"Stop it," I whispered.

He glanced at me. "Don't like hearing the truth?"

"You have no idea of the truth, or what Nexus is capable of." Crap, I heard the emotion in my voice.

Silence filled the car.

"Nexus?"

Shit, I should have kept my mouth shut.

"Are you in trouble?" Liam asked. "Are they forcing you to do this?"

God. I looked out the side window. Heaven help me if he started being nice to me. "Just drop it."

"Penn—"

"We both know that isn't truly my name."

I met his gaze. The blue hit me like a laser beam.

"There are things I can't discuss." I shook my head. "You should just worry about yourself."

His hands flexed on the wheel. Then he pulled into a parking space just down from the Woolworth Building.

"So, they are forcing you."

"No." *Dammit.* I got out of the car and started walking.

"Penn—" He grabbed my arm. "Talk to me. I can help you."

God, he really was a good guy. "You need to help yourself." I yanked away and strode down the sidewalk. I felt him bearing down behind me.

My burner phone beeped and I pulled it out.

My heart clenched. It was a message from Doyle.

I read the message, frowned, and typed. *Why not money?*

I'd assumed Doyle would ask Liam for an exorbitant amount of money.

I don't want money. Get me what I want.

Stopping, I sucked in a breath and swiveled. I lifted my chin. "To make sure the photos stay secret, you need to sign a piece of property at Borden Street in the Bronx over to Nexus Corp."

Liam stilled and cocked his head. "That property is key to the Borden Project."

I swallowed. "That's a requirement. Nexus doesn't want money, only the property. If you don't comply—"

Liam leaned closer. "How's it feel to be a blackmailer?"

I made myself hold his gaze. "You don't understand."

"Oh, I understand perfectly. No fucking deal. I'll find a way to shield my family, my father can cop the consequences." He brushed past me and into the building.

I blew out a breath. *No.* Jake's life and freedom depended on Nexus getting what they wanted from Liam.

Then I tapped into my phone.

He said no.

I started to slide the phone away. I had to see this through.

My phone beeped.

Then we'll have to offer him more persuasion.

A prickle ran down my spine. What the hell did that mean?

7

PLAN'S CHANGED

Liam

L iam rose. "Thank you, David. Productive, as always." He held out his hand.

The businessman shook Liam's hand. "And you're as wily as ever, Kensington. Somehow you always talk me out of more, and I'm always happy about it."

Liam smiled. Beside them, Penn rose, collecting her things.

"And Ms. Channing," David said with a smile. "You were efficient and competent, like all of Liam's staff."

"Thank you, Mr. Warner." She glanced at Liam. "Mr. Kensington only hires the best."

Liam hid his snort.

His anger was still bubbling under his skin, his mind ticking over. Why the hell did the blackmailers want that land in the Bronx?

It was an old warehouse, crumbling and ready for demolition.

Penn moved ahead of him and his gaze dropped down her athletic body and tight curves. His jaw clenched. He was angry at himself.

The woman couldn't be trusted.

He wanted her gone from Kensington Group, but his hands were tied until he found a way to deal with his blackmailers. He released a breath. He'd sent Vander Norcross a message last night. The private investigator had promised to dig up what he could. But now, Liam had more to give Vander—the name Nexus and the fact that the bastards wanted the Bronx property. He needed to call Vander.

The elevator doors closed him and Penn in together.

"My employers are unhappy that you aren't taking our demands more seriously," she said.

Clearly, she'd been in contact with them.

"You mean threats?"

Her face was so cool, so unconcerned.

He stepped closer. "Children will be dragged through the mud. Do you even care? Are you all ice?"

He thought for a second he saw a flicker in her eyes.

Then her chin lifted. "Are you going to sign over the property? Do it, and this all goes away."

"Fuck you, Penn." His chest was heaving, anger alive in his veins.

She licked her lips and his gaze dropped downward.

Liam felt a sharp tug in his gut. How the fuck could he be attracted to his blackmailer?

The elevator dinged and the doors opened. With a muscle working in his jaw, Liam stepped back. He straightened his suit jacket and held the door.

Penn stepped out.

The richly detailed lobby of the Woolworth Building was an assault on the senses. It was filled with mosaics, gold leaf, sculptures, and other architectural flourishes.

"I need the ladies'." She didn't look at him as she strode away.

He couldn't stop himself drinking in her tight ass under her fitted, gray trousers.

"Fuck." He pulled out his cell phone.

There were several messages from Mav and Zane, checking in. Liam went through some emails and deleted one from his father without reading it.

He punched in a number.

"Vander Norcross," a deep voice said.

"Vander, it's Liam Kensington."

"Liam. I've had my tech guy Ace running some searches, but you didn't give us much to go on."

"I have more today. The blackmailers made their demands. They want me to sign over a property in the Bronx to them."

"Anything special about it?"

"Not that I know of. It's an old warehouse."

"Okay, text me the address and we'll look into it. Ace has run this Penn Channing. She doesn't exist beyond a few layers. It's an alias."

Liam muttered a curse. "I guessed as much. She said the name of the group. Nexus."

"Nexus." Vander was silent a moment. "Name rings a bell. Let me see what Ace can find."

"I'll see if I can get some more information out of Penn."

"Tread carefully, Liam. Once I can dig up something on these blackmailers and the land they want, I'll be in touch."

"Thanks, Vander."

Penn still wasn't back. Liam frowned and slid the phone away, then followed the signs to the restrooms.

A moment later, he saw her come out, but she hadn't spotted him yet.

She sagged against the marble wall for a second, her shoulders slumped.

Liam stilled, looking at the weariness on her face.

A woman carrying a heavy weight.

Shit. One voice in his head told him to walk away. To collect everything he knew about her, then hand it over to the police.

But there was another voice in his head as well. Was she in trouble? Was she being forced to do this? She didn't always act the way a blackmailer should.

He'd just seen Monroe blackmailed into stealing from Zane to save her brother.

Was Penn in a similar predicament?

"Problem?" he asked.

She jerked and straightened away from the wall. Her face smoothed out. "No."

"You want to tell me how you fell into a life of crime and blackmail?"

Her eye twitched. "No." She walked past him toward the front doors.

He followed her. "If you're in trouble, you need to tell me."

She met his gaze, and gave a quick shake of her head. "You're persistent as hell."

"You don't reach my level of success by being lazy or by giving up."

They exited and were assailed by sunlight and the cool air. Somewhere nearby, a car horn honked.

"Let's just get back to the office." She started down the sidewalk toward the car. "You need to organize for the deed to be signed over for that piece of land, and then your life can go on as normal."

Liam dodged around some other people on the sidewalk and grabbed her arm. "Penn—"

There was a loud screech of tires. Then more honking horns.

They both looked up.

Time seemed to slow down.

A black sedan sped closer. The back window opened.

For a millisecond, Liam didn't realize what he was seeing.

It was a gun barrel.

"Everybody get down!" Penn yelled.

There was a roar of gunfire.

A body slammed into Liam's, driving him to the ground. His back hit the pavement, Penn's body stretched out on top of his.

"Stay down!" she yelled.

Bullets hit the building behind them.

Glass shattered. People screamed.

"Are you okay?" she asked. "Are you hit?"

"No. I'm fine."

Before Liam could process more than that, she leaped up.

He saw the sedan screech to a halt in the street. Cars swerved and people slammed on their brakes. Then the sedan started to reverse backward toward them. Gunfire was still spraying from the back seat.

They were sitting ducks.

Suddenly, Penn yanked a black handgun from her bag.

Liam froze. *What the hell?*

She aimed the gun with two hands, and calmly fired on the car.

He sat up. She held the gun like he'd seen cops do it. Her face was set and focused, no trace of the adrenaline that had to be pounding through her body.

The sedan stopped, then its tires screeched as it shot forward again, racing away.

Penn cursed and lowered the gun to her side.

Liam rose, keeping his gaze locked on her.

Her face was calm, and she scanned the area around them carefully.

"More secrets, Ms. Channing?"

Her gaze flicked to his. Then she reached out and grabbed his arm. "Come on. It isn't safe."

Around them, people were screaming and crying. She pulled him down the sidewalk.

"You'd better start telling me what the fuck is going on," he said.

She opened her mouth.

"No more lies this time."

Penn scanned around. "Fine. I'll explain, but for now, get in the car."

Aspen

The atmosphere inside the car was tense.

As Liam drove, I scanned ahead and behind for the black sedan.

When Doyle had texted me that they were going to give Liam some encouragement, this was *not* what I'd imagined.

The asshole had almost killed us.

My mind flashed with a picture of Liam's bullet-riddled body sprawled on the sidewalk, and my belly clenched.

Hell, no. I couldn't, wouldn't, let him get hurt.

This felt a lot more personal than just doing my job, but I couldn't examine that right now.

Maybe I shouldn't ever examine it.

Liam took a corner fast, but then we hit traffic and slowed. A cab cut in front of us.

Hell, I just wanted Liam safely back in his office.

"So, you aren't a blackmailer or marketing assistant, I assume."

I didn't look at him.

"Who are you?" he demanded.

"We'll talk at your office. I want you off the street and safe."

Liam Kensington was smart. He'd already been

adding things up, and I could see it all working behind his blue eyes.

Grabbing my phone, I tapped in a message to Erica. *Plan's changed. I need to tell Kensington what's going on.*

Next, I messaged Doyle. *WTF? You could've killed me and Kensington.*

Did Doyle know that I'd returned fire? Would it make him suspicious of me?

I should have maintained my cover, but I sure as hell wasn't going to die, or let them kill Liam.

My phone pinged with a message.

It was a warning. That's all.

I tapped in furiously.

The assholes were aiming to kill. Hire better people.

I glanced at Liam.

His body was tense, his jaw tight. He turned his head and met my gaze.

"I'm tired of lies and secrets, Penn."

"Sometimes my whole life seems like lies and secrets." I tried to relax my shoulders. "You get used to it."

The Kensington Group building appeared and Liam drove into the parking garage.

He parked the sexy, little Aston, and as soon as I got out, he grabbed my arm and towed me toward the elevator.

"I can walk myself. I've been doing it for several years now."

He shot me one searing look and I closed my mouth.

Liam Kensington was really, really angry.

We exited on the executive floor and he kept a hold of

my arm as we headed for his office. A male assistant appeared.

"Mr. Kensington, I put Mr. Crown in the main boardroom for your meeting."

"Something came up. Give him my apologies and reschedule."

The assistant's eyes widened, and he shot a curious glance in my direction.

We sailed right past Eleanor's desk.

His personal assistant rose. "Liam—?"

"Hold all my calls, Eleanor."

The older woman shot me a narrow stare.

Then Liam slammed his office door closed.

He released me and strode toward his desk. He stripped off his suit jacket with jerky moves and tossed it over the guest chair.

I took a second to admire him, even though his blue striped shirt was a little rumpled, he looked delicious.

He spun, his hands on his lean hips. "Talk."

"I suspect that you're so used to giving orders that you don't even realize how bossy and supercilious you sound."

His gaze narrowed. He started toward me.

My pulse spiked. "Liam—"

He kept coming, fire in his eyes.

I backed up.

He kept coming and my shoulder blades hit the wall.

"Who. Are. You?"

My brain whirred. Erica hadn't responded. I needed to talk with her first. Everything had gone to hell and I wasn't sure what the next step should be. "I can't share that with you just yet."

He grabbed my chin. "Do you ever give a straight answer?"

I met his gaze. "Yes. Most of the time, actually." I sighed. "I want to tell you, but I can't yet."

His fingers stroked my skin and I shivered.

There was something else in his gaze now.

"You like that?" he asked quietly.

"It doesn't matter if I do or don't, getting involved with you is a very bad idea. For both of us."

His head leaned closer. "I have no doubt about that."

"Liam," I breathed. His nearness was sending my body haywire. I'd always prided myself on never losing control over a man. Ever. Why did this one affect me so much?

"Do you know what it's like to feel so drawn to a woman, so attracted, and realize I don't know a bloody thing about her?"

I heard the frustration in his voice. "I'm sorry."

He studied my face. "I actually think you are, but it doesn't change anything. I want to know who you are and what the fuck is going on."

"I can't. Yet." *Come on, Erica.*

Liam's grip tightened.

I pushed his hand away and put some distance between us.

He reached for me again and I automatically blocked his move.

He reached again and I knocked his arm aside.

Those beautiful blue eyes sharpened. I saw the killer

businessman in them—assessing for strengths and weaknesses.

He grabbed my shirt, and I gripped the front of his. We moved in a half circle, like two predators ready to fight.

I aimed a light punch at his flat stomach, but he blocked my hit, surprising me.

My other arm swung up, and his hand snapped out, circling my wrist.

He'd read my moves, blocked them.

"You have some moves," I said.

"As do you."

He backed me up a step and my butt hit the edge of his desk.

"I didn't expect you to," I said.

"Do you think billionaires are too busy breathing rarefied air and buying designer suits?" He arched a brow.

He leaned into me, that hard male body tantalizingly close. And he smelled so good.

I cocked my head. "Um, pretty much."

Then my phone vibrated.

I slid it out and saw the message from Erica. *Finally.*

I'll do whatever you think is best. I just want Jake back.

I pressed a hand to Liam's chest. "Back up, Liam."

"No."

Stubborn. Fine.

I lifted my chin. "My name isn't Penn Channing."

"I'd already guessed that," he said dryly.

"Penn isn't a total lie. I use it sometimes as a nickname." I pulled in a breath. "My name is Aspen Chandler." I felt his attention sharpen on me. "I was hired by one of your employees, who also happens to be a friend of mine. Her husband was kidnapped by a crime group called Nexus. All we want is her husband back safely. Nexus wanted to use her to get close to you, but I made myself a better option. I'm a private investigator."

8

NOT SURE THIS IS A GOOD IDEA

Liam

*W*hat. The. Hell?

Penn's revelation, or should he say, Aspen's, rocketed through Liam.

She was a private investigator.

She wasn't a criminal.

She wasn't a blackmailer.

She hadn't betrayed him.

"I'm undercover with Nexus, and—"

"Quiet." He dragged in a breath. "You're a private investigator?"

She nodded. "I'm working for Erica Knox. They abducted her husband, Jake."

Liam was somehow angry and elated all at the same time.

"I am sorry, Liam." Aspen's eyes were earnest. "I never wanted to hurt you, but there's a man's life on the line—"

Liam lowered his head and kissed her.

She froze at the touch of his lips, then she moaned and her hands sank into his hair.

He yanked her closer, tongue plunging into her mouth. She tasted so, so good—sweet, with a touch of spice.

Nudging her legs apart, he stepped between them. He resented any distance between them.

Their mouths slanted together, and he slid an arm around her and pulled her closer. Her breasts were flush against his chest.

She gasped into his mouth. Damn, he wanted to hear that exact sound when he was deep inside her.

Their tongues tangled, a private little war, both of them trying to get as much of each other as they could. One of her hands tugged his tie loose, then her mouth was on his neck.

Damn.

Desire was like molten metal in his veins—scorching hot. It all headed south to his throbbing cock.

Aspen licked his skin, then bit down. Liam groaned, gripped her hips and pulled her closer. As his cock pressed against her core, she moaned.

He hated the layers of clothes between them.

That's when the ringing sound registered. For a second, he thought it was just his overwhelmed senses.

Then he heard Penn curse.

She pushed him back a step, and pulled her cell phone out of her pocket.

"Erica, I'm here."

Dragging in air, Liam stepped back.

Penn slipped off the table and started pacing. "Yes, I'm with him now." She turned away, murmuring to her friend. No doubt updating Erica on what had happened.

Aspen Chandler.

Penn suited her, but so did Aspen. Liam leaned back against his desk, trying to get his raging erection under control.

"We're at Liam's office." She flicked a glance his way, and her gaze dropped. When she noted the bulge in the front of his suit pants, her cheeks turned pink.

A private investigator who blushed. Fascinating.

"Are you going to mention what we were doing?" Liam asked.

She shot him a look. "Yes, I promise we're fine. No, this isn't your fault. Erica, you need to stay calm."

Liam crossed his ankles. "Please ask her to come up here. We'll discuss a path forward."

Aspen turned to face him. "Liam wants you to come up here. Yes, we'll see you soon." She ended the call. "She's on her way up."

Liam inclined his head.

"We'll bring you up to speed on the investigation, and then we need to decide on a path forward."

"Penn... Or should I call you Aspen now?"

"It needs to be Penn in public."

"So, Penn in public, and Aspen in private." He pushed away from the desk. "We need to talk. About what just happened on my desk."

Her cheeks went pink again. "That can't happen again."

"Oh, it's going to happen again. Repeatedly."

She held up a hand. "You are a person of interest in my investigation—"

"I'm not involved with this crime gang."

"I know that, but you're their focus. I need to get Jake back, all while I keep you safe, and bring down Nexus."

"Bring down Nexus?"

She swallowed. "I never wanted to see you or your family get hurt, and if I can, I want to stop them from hurting anyone else. My first priority is getting Jake home safely, but in the meantime, I've been collecting everything I can on Nexus. My plan is to turn it over to the authorities."

God, he'd been so wrong about her.

"I can't afford to muddy the waters, or my head." She blew out a breath. "And you're a man designed to turn a woman's head, and better judgment, to mush."

He smiled. "Glad to see I'm not alone. You make my control evaporate with a single look."

"Liam—"

"I get it, Aspen. A man's in danger, and you have a job to do." He stepped closer and heard her sharp breath. "But I know you feel this...connection. I feel it, you feel it. I'm not walking away from that. And I'm also not a man to stand by while assholes try to take advantage of me and my family. So, I will be involved with this investigation. Every step of the way."

She stared at him.

The phone on his desk buzzed, and Liam circled the desk and hit the button. "Yes?"

"Liam, Mrs. Knox from Human Resources is here to

see you," Eleanor said. "She doesn't have an appointment."

"That's fine, please send her in."

A moment later, Erica entered Liam's office. She wore a flowing, floral dress with knee-high boots, and Liam had never seen the redhead look so pale.

"Mr. Kensington, I'm so, so sorry. I never wanted to hurt you." She clasped her hands together.

He moved toward her. "It's all right, Erica. I'm so sorry about your husband. Unfortunately, my success makes me a target." He took her hands. "I'm sorry you got caught up in this."

Tears welled in her eyes. "I just want Jake back safely."

"We're going to make that happen."

"I see you officially met Aspen," Erica said, with a small, watery smile.

Liam smiled in return and looked at Aspen. "I did. It came as a surprise, although I was very pleased to know that she wasn't actually a blackmailer."

"Nexus is dangerous," Aspen said. "We have to find a way to get Jake free."

Liam nodded. "And I don't want those photos to get released. If we work together, I think we might be able to sort this out."

Aspen glanced at Erica, then back at him. "This gang's already killed, Liam, and they're not afraid to do it again."

Liam's gut hardened. "I got that when they shot at us today." He met her gaze. "Aspen, we'll need to work very, *very* closely together."

Behind Erica's back, Aspen shot him a look.

Aspen

I watched Erica leave and turned back to Liam.

He was standing by the windows, lean body silhouetted by the light, and Manhattan a magnificent backdrop.

He looked every inch the billionaire businessman.

He also looked edible.

I pushed the punch of simmering desire down low. I couldn't afford to let the attraction grow.

I had to bring Jake home and find a way to bring Nexus down.

"So," I said.

He turned. "So."

I dropped into one of the guest chairs in front of his big desk. "We need to work out why Nexus wants that land."

Liam touched the phone on his desk. "Eleanor, pull the file on the Borden property in the Bronx, please."

"Sure thing, Liam."

"It's a decrepit warehouse." He leaned a hip against his desk. "The land is valuable, of course, but I'm guessing Nexus isn't in construction or development."

I frowned, tapping my nails on the arm of the chair. "No. They usually go for a quick win, like blackmail and demanding money." My stomach churned.

There was a knock at the door, and Eleanor entered.

"Here's the file." Liam's assistant glanced at me, her gaze the perfect blend of curious and suspicious.

"Thank you," Liam said.

After Eleanor left, he sat at his desk and flicked through the file. I circled around and leaned over his shoulder.

"The warehouse originally dates from the Prohibition era. Through the years it's been home to various businesses; the last one was a shoe factory."

I shook my head. I couldn't see any clear connection. "What could they possibly want with it?"

"I've contacted a highly recommended private investigator—"

"No," I said. "We can't risk bringing more people into this."

"He could help. Vander knows what he's doing, and he won't talk."

"Wait." I stilled. "Vander *Norcross*?"

Liam nodded.

My mouth dropped open. The man was a legend. He'd been commander of some covert special operations teams in the military before he'd returned to civilian life and started Norcross Security and Investigations in San Francisco. The stories I'd heard whispered about him couldn't possibly all be true. The man knew players on both sides of the law all across the country.

I was a baby minnow PI, and Vander Norcross was a big, bad Great White shark.

I chewed on it for a second. "Okay. He might be able to dig up something we can't."

Liam's lips quirked. "I wasn't asking for your permission."

I stepped closer. "We're working together, Kensington, but this is *my* investigation."

He rose from his chair, the toes of his shoes brushing mine.

"And this is my life. I will protect my family."

"I don't want anyone hurt, but ultimately, I need to bring Jake home. And if I can, stop Doyle."

"Doyle?"

I blew out a breath. "He's the leader of Nexus. Kristoff Doyle. Just a shadowy figure, who doesn't reveal his true identity. He's left a string of shattered lives behind while taking the money and disappearing into darkness."

Liam stared at me until I wanted to fidget.

His hand cupped my shoulder. Such a simple, innocent touch, but I felt it everywhere.

"This sounds personal," he said quietly.

I dropped my gaze. "I'm doing my job."

"Has this Doyle hurt you?"

I tried to pull away. "No."

"No secrets, Aspen. Who is he?"

"Liam—"

"Tell me." His face was close to mine.

"I don't know him, but people like him destroyed my family." The words burst out of me like poison.

Both Liam's hands curled around my shoulders. "I'm sorry."

I heard the sympathy in his quiet words. "I was fourteen. My father owned a small finance company. He invested other people's money. Some people dragged him into a Ponzi scheme."

"Shit," Liam muttered.

"The scandal broke. People, a lot of them our friends and neighbors, lost their life savings." I thought of the young boy next door, Anthony. He'd been a friend, until his father had committed suicide during all this mess. Anthony had looked at me with such hatred afterward. "My father went down, but the people who'd worked with him disappeared. My mother disintegrated under the strain. Instead of the nice life in her big house with the support of a well-off husband, she found herself a single mom of three girls, reviled by the community, and with no way to support herself. My mother couldn't cope, and I had two little sisters who needed raising."

"How did you cope, Aspen?"

"I did what I had to do. Helped care for my sisters, and studied harder. I had to leave my private school, and the kids at the new school loved having a juicy, new target."

The bullying had been relentless.

"I get it," he said quietly. "My parents' marriage disintegrated slowly, publicly, and spectacularly. My father had numerous affairs, before being caught with an actress half his age, having sex in a car. My mother didn't cope well. She lost it, and loved spewing her rage at my father in interviews. And the bullies sniff out any blood in the water, as do the press."

"I'm sorry." I shook my head. "It's all in the past."

"Is it?" His gaze was piercing. "I sense you became an investigator because you wanted to stop things like this."

"I just want to help people."

"Do you?"

"Quit with the psychoanalysis. We need to stop Nexus and save Jake, *that's* our focus."

"Well, I think we need to take a look at the warehouse."

"Agreed." I turned all the facts over in my head. "And I need to buy some time with Doyle. Let him think I'm working you, and if he gives me a few days, I can convince you to give him what he wants."

Liam frowned. "Will he go for it?"

I straightened. "I'll make him."

"I have an idea." He stepped closer, and fingered my hair.

"Hey, hands off." I slapped his hands away.

"Tell Doyle we're sleeping together."

My heart tripped. "What?"

"You heard me."

"You're sleeping with the woman who's blackmailing you?"

Liam smiled. "A good lie always has an element of truth, doesn't it, Aspen? Tell him that I'm bored with models and socialites. Tired of the glittering, shiny party-goers. Tell him that I'm hopelessly in lust with you because you're different and you intrigue me."

I wasn't sure exactly which part of that was real and which was a lie.

"I'm not sure this is a good idea," I said.

"Do you have a better one?"

Aspen

I sat on the couch in Liam's office, the phone to my ear, waiting for Doyle to pick up.

My belly was full of nerves.

This was a bad idea.

I needed to buy time by convincing Doyle that Liam and I were sleeping together.

Liam paced nearby. He had his hands in his pockets, a scowl on his face.

"Did he sign the deed?" Doyle's raspy voice said in my ear.

"No. But he will."

"Channing—"

"Listen. I've got this. I just need a few more days and I'll have him doing *anything* I want."

Liam glanced over at me. His blue gaze hit me, and I felt a zing.

"Explain," Doyle demanded.

I swallowed. "The guy's hot for me. Obsessed."

Liam sat beside me.

I heard a sound of surprise from Doyle.

That's it. Take the bait.

"You're sleeping with him?" Doyle asked.

"Yes." I laughed, putting as much sultry into it as I could. "Believe me, it's no hardship to tear up the sheets with a man who looks like Liam Kensington."

Liam gripped my knee and squeezed. I shot him a look, and pushed his hand away.

"I'd rock your world," he murmured.

I rolled my eyes.

"He's sleeping with the woman who's blackmailing him?" Doyle asked skeptically.

"Oh, I'm sure he thinks he has the upper hand." I shot a pointed look at Liam.

The man didn't bother to hide his grin.

"But he's hungry for me. I think he's bored with the society beauties and long-legged models. I intrigue him."

Liam touched my face and our gazes locked.

I felt so damn much. It was more than a little terrifying. "Give me a couple of days, and I'll have him eating out of the palm of my hand."

"Hmm, I guess I can give you a few days." There was a significant pause. "He hasn't swayed you with a better deal, has he, Penn?"

I laughed. "No, but maybe I should let him."

"I'll be watching you. You have three days. Get it done."

The line went dead.

"Well?" Liam asked.

"I'm not sure he's one-hundred-percent convinced, but he's given me three days to get you to sign the deed."

Liam nodded. "So we have three days to find out why Nexus wants that land, find a way to lure out Doyle, and rescue Jake Knox."

"He's suspicious, Liam. He said he'd be watching."

"So, I need to look like a madly infatuated man."

I raised a brow, hiding my true reaction, because I wondered what it would be like to have a man like Liam infatuated with me. "Think you're up for the task?"

"I think I can manage." He rose. "Especially since I can't keep my hands off you."

"Don't let reality and fiction blur, Kensington."

"How about I do something out of character, and escape work early with my new lady love."

"We can't be seen in public, Liam. If we were photographed together—"

He nodded. "Someone might discover that you're actually a private investigator moonlighting as a white-collar criminal, and blow your cover." He stroked his chin. "We'll go to my place. We can canoodle by the windows for anyone who's watching."

I considered. "That'll work."

"Good." He grabbed his jacket and slipped it on. "All right, Ms. Irresistible, let's go."

My eyes narrowed. "Are you making fun of me?"

His eyebrows rose. "How?"

"I'm hardly irresistible." I was well aware that I was attractive, and I had my strengths, but I'd never use irresistible as an adjective to describe me.

That maddening smile appeared on his face. "Women always profess that men don't understand what makes them tick, but the same is true for the reverse."

I frowned, confused.

He leaned closer, that sexy scent of his hitting me.

"You have no idea what I find irresistible, Aspen. I can't wait to show you."

I pressed a palm to his chest, felt the warm skin under the fine fabric. "Remember, us being in lust is just for show."

He headed for the door, sending me a charming smile. "Speak for yourself."

When Liam informed Eleanor that he and I were

leaving for the day, his assistant looked like he'd beaned her with her desk phone.

He showed me to his Aston Martin, and soon, we were driving to his place. It took me about thirty seconds to spot the tail.

"We're being followed." I glanced casually in the side mirror.

Liam flicked a glance at the rearview mirror. "White Ford."

"That's it."

We stopped at a red light. Suddenly, Liam leaned over, grabbed me and kissed me.

Oh, God. I forgot my name. He was too potent.

The light changed, and a horn honked behind us.

My pulse was still racing as he drove onward.

We finally reached his place. I knew he lived by Madison Square Park, not far from my apartment, but I wasn't exactly prepared.

He pulled up at a gorgeous, Neo-Gothic building on Fifth Avenue. A valet driver in a suit rushed out to meet us and opened my door.

"Welcome." The man smiled at me.

Liam circled the car. "Good afternoon, Marc."

"Hi, Mr. Kensington."

Liam handed over the keys, and then ushered me inside. He whisked me through the lobby, and I got the impression of brown marble and gold accents, and then we were in a private elevator. The building had twenty-one floors.

"Which floor are you on?" I asked.

"The top three."

The top *three?* "Penthouse?"

He nodded.

When the door opened, I stepped inside and tried to keep my jaw from hitting the floor. Holy cow, I'd interacted with a few wealthy people before, but this was next-level.

"Wow. You're really, really rich."

"I am." He set his keys on a side table.

My first impression was space. The ceilings were high, the windows were huge. The floors were a pale wood, and the furnishings were all shades of cream. God, I'd spill something on that pristine upholstery. I knew it.

I could see the Flatiron Building and the park, the city beyond it. Liam strode across the huge living area to the kitchen. He set the file on the Bronx property on the lake-sized island made of white marble, veined with gray.

"Should we stand on the terrace?" he suggested. "If anyone is watching, they might spot us. We can give them a show."

I glanced out at the terrace. It was walled in with sleek outdoor furniture. It looked private.

"Not that terrace, the upper deck," he said. "More chance of being seen."

"You have two terraces?"

"Yes." That wicked smile.

"You're enjoying this."

"Being close to you is no hardship." He echoed my own words. "Glass of wine?"

I nodded. I wouldn't normally drink, but I needed it to settle my nerves.

He pulled a bottle of something from his huge

Subzero refrigerator. It took him a second to open it, then he grabbed two glasses from a cupboard. He poured the pretty gold liquid into the glass and then poured one for himself too.

"Come on." He handed me a glass, then took my hand.

His hands weren't soft. I found it surprising that he had calluses. He led me up some stairs, and I stared at the huge, draping chandelier in the void space. He opened the doors onto a huge terrace.

"This is incredible," I breathed.

There was a fire pit off to one side, surrounded by comfy chairs. Some sun loungers lay on the other side of the terrace, along with a large carved statue made of black stone.

But the most impressive thing was the view of downtown. It was breathtaking.

"Do you have a pool?"

He pointed over the glass railing. I glanced down at the pool on the level below.

I wanted to weep. I loved my apartment, but I'd trade it for Liam's place in an instant. Although, I'd definitely add more plants if I lived here.

We stood at the railing, and I stared at the Kensington Group building in the distance, then I scanned the street far below.

"Can you see anyone?" he asked.

I glanced around casually, like I was taking in the view. "Not from up here, but they're likely there, somewhere, with a telephoto lens aimed our way." I sipped the wine, then moaned. "Oh my God, this is so good."

"Glad you like it."

"What is it?" If I memorized the name, maybe I could grab a bottle next time I needed wine.

"It's Château d'Yquem."

I paused. "That sounds expensive."

"About five hundred dollars for this bottle. But it gets more expensive depending on the vintage."

I choked on my next sip. "Seriously?"

"Drink up." He leaned in, his fingers dancing over my temple. "You really think someone's watching?"

"Probably."

"Well, in that case—" He took the wineglasses and set them on the table.

"Liam—" I pressed my hands to his chest.

"Relax."

He stroked my cheek. Desperate, I grabbed onto anything to distract me. "Why do you have calluses on your hands?"

"You expected them to be soft?"

"Yes."

"I worked construction in college to help pay my way."

I blinked. "Why? Your family is wealthy."

"My father is prone to tantrums. He liked to cut me off periodically, depending on his moods. Especially if I didn't follow his exact wishes. I never knew if I'd have money to pay rent each month."

"Liam, that's terrible."

"We've all had things to cope with in our lives. Tough times. I'm well aware people have had it far tougher than me. Those situations, they forge us, make us stronger. It can't always be smooth sailing. Besides, I've learned that the best stuff usually arrives after the storm." He pulled me closer. "I'm going to kiss you now."

I glanced over his shoulder. "Is someone watching?"

"I've no idea."

His mouth closed on mine.

9

HE SMELLED LIKE SIN

Liam

L iam pulled Aspen closer, sliding a hand up to cup the back of her head.

Damn, she tasted so good. A delicious temptation.

She made a sound close to a whimper, pressing into him. Moving his lips on hers, he tried to keep some control.

He should've known better.

The touch of her, the taste of her, it was like a damn drug.

And he was willingly addicted.

She tasted like Aspen and wine. Everything about this woman sung to his senses.

More. *Take more.*

He pulled back for a second, absorbing her flushed cheeks and swollen lips, then he fused his mouth to hers again.

She made a hungry sound. His tongue delved into

her mouth, and she met him stroke for stroke. His groan vibrated in his chest and he deepened the kiss.

Liam slid one hand up her body, shaping her rib cage. He pulled her shirt free of her trousers, then his hand was on skin.

"God." She ripped her mouth free. Her breathing was fast, and she pressed her forehead to his chest. "You should come with a danger warning for women."

He stroked a hand down her back, trying to get a lock on the raging desire twisting through him.

"That should be enough of a show," he said.

"A show. Right." The light leaked from her eyes.

"Aspen." He grabbed her hand.

She tugged. "We should—"

He yanked her close, and she bumped against his chest. "You think lust like that can be faked?"

She just stared at him.

"You ever just let loose, Ms. Chandler?"

"No." She shook her head. "Especially not when I'm working."

"That kiss was real. And I'll show you more."

"We are *not* getting personally involved."

He smiled. "We already are."

"Your persistence isn't cute."

"And yet, your pulse is racing."

He tugged her inside. His phone dinged, a reminder from his calendar. Aspen's phone dinged at the same time.

With a huff, she pulled her phone out. Liam checked his. *Crap.* With everything going on tonight, he'd forgotten the Wounded Warriors fundraiser tonight.

Aspen tapped furiously on her phone.

"Everything okay?" he asked.

She rolled her eyes. "I'm refereeing an argument between my sisters." She stabbed at the phone and pressed it to her ear. "I don't care who cooks dinner, as long as someone does." A pause. "No, Briar. Tell Juno I said no as well. Uh-huh. No." She growled. "I swear to God, you two are nineteen, not five, sort it out." Aspen rolled her eyes again. "I love you, too."

"Your sisters live with you?" he asked.

She nodded. "They're both at college here in the city. I have a spare room. They drive me crazy most of the time."

And it was clear she loved them to pieces.

"Aspen, I have a charity dinner tonight."

"Okay. You should take some security with you. There's no telling what else Doyle has up his sleeve to 'convince' you to give him what he wants."

"A good idea. I'll take you."

She froze. "What?"

"Come as my date. We'll kill two birds. This will be convincing for Doyle, showing him that I'm infatuated with my beautiful, wily blackmailer. And you can protect me."

"I can't be seen at an event, Liam. If I'm identified—"

"So wear a wig. Surely you private-investigator types are good with disguises. Besides, if you wear a fabulous dress, no one will be looking at your face."

Her nose wrinkled. "That's sexist as hell. Besides, I don't have a fabulous dress."

"I'll take care of the dress."

He saw the battle on her face. "Okay, fine. Just because it's best for the investigation."

"Great. Give me your address. I'll have a dress delivered, then I'll pick you up at seven PM."

"No. I'll meet you there. Where is it?"

Shit, she was so stubborn.

He thought about what she'd shared of her childhood. He suspected Aspen Chandler had been forced to grow up far too young. Even now, she was still caring for her sisters. What she'd gone through had made her strong, tough. Maybe too tough sometimes.

"It's at Gotham Hall," he said.

"Of course, it is."

The impressive neoclassical building was in Midtown, and had once housed a bank. Now it was renowned for hosting exclusive weddings and events.

"And no more kissing." There was a glint in her eye.

"We'll see."

Liam

A few hours later, Liam found himself in his tuxedo, sipping Scotch in the opulent grandeur of the grand ballroom at Gotham Hall.

The gilded ceiling soared overhead, with its stained-glass centerpiece. The granite walls were lit up with blue light, and impressive columns at the end of the oval hall just added to the sense of splendor. A dance floor and band stood at one end, and several high tables were dotted around the center of the space, lit with golden lights. The bar and food tables were stretched along the sides of the room.

Liam thought he'd found a private corner, but people kept stopping by for a chitchat. Or the hopes to make a time to meet him to discuss a business deal.

He glanced around, but he wasn't seeing the fancy party, he was thinking of Nexus. Out there, somewhere, stalking like a predator.

He was going to help Aspen and bring them down.

He wasn't letting those photos hurt his family, and he was making sure Jake was back with his wife.

Liam glanced at his watch. Where was Aspen? She was late.

He wished that Mav and Zane were here. Zane had declined to come. No doubt he was snuggled up with Monroe. Mav was probably locked in his lab, cooking up his next million-dollar invention.

Actually, it was good that they weren't here. Aspen would generate too many questions that Liam didn't want to answer. He didn't want to drag his friends into danger.

He'd keep them clear of this mess.

He heard whispers, sensed a change in the crowd.

He turned.

And the air locked in his chest.

Aspen strode in through the imposing brass doors like she owned the room.

Her hair was a cascade of deep wine-red waves that fell just past her bare shoulders. Long, sparkly earrings dangled from her ears.

Her dress was black, but that didn't begin to describe it. He'd asked his tailor to send a knockout dress over. He'd never asked that before and Alessandro had been giddy at the prospect. Now, Liam was either going to tip the man, or kill him.

The dress was strapless and fitted her torso well with a tiny strip of mesh at her waist. He let his gaze drift over her toned arms. The black fabric of the dress shimmered with sparkles, looking like velvet sprinkled with diamond chips. Her skirt was full, falling to the floor.

Fuck. He felt himself get hard.

She scanned the space, found him. A mysterious, female smile crossed her face.

She started toward him.

That's when he realized that one side of the full skirt had a slit all the way to the top of one, toned thigh.

Liam's cock grew harder. Yes, Alessandro was a dead man.

He sensed people watching her, seeing all that golden skin and slender leg. She'd painted her eyes dark like smoke, her lips an intriguing bronze.

She lifted a hand to tuck a strand of hair behind her ear and he saw a tattoo along the outside of her forearm. Words written in a flowing script. He desperately wanted to know what they said. Hell, he wanted to know everything about her.

He set his drink down and pushed through the crowd to meet her.

"Hi," she murmured.

He couldn't form any words. He slid an arm around

her, fighting the urge to brand her so everyone would know exactly who she belonged to.

Her lips twitched. "I take it you like the dress?"

He touched his lips to hers. He heard more frenzied whispers in the crowd.

"No, I like what's under the dress."

Aspen

I couldn't believe I was standing in the middle of a swanky party at Gotham Hall, wearing a designer dress and being held in the arms of a billionaire.

Me. Aspen Chandler. Small-time private investigator.

People were staring at us, but right then and there, all I could see was Liam.

He looked outrageously sexy in his tux—it fit him like a lover's touch. He smelled like sin. That sandalwood scent was designed to fire up a woman's ovaries and shut down rational thought.

He pulled me closer and I felt a hard bulge nudge my belly. My mouth went dry. "You really like the dress."

"Give me a minute."

Damn if I didn't like knowing that I affected him like this. A man who could take his pick of any of the gorgeous women in the room.

"So, we have a drink, circle the room, then get out of here," I said.

The less time I was with him, the less chance I would slip up and forget to be a professional.

"We have to dance."

I narrowed my eyes. A few couples were on the shiny dance floor where the band was playing.

"I don't dance, Kensington."

"Don't worry, I'll lead. You'll be in good hands."

"You've been warned."

"Sir? Ma'am? Would you like some champagne?"

We turned our heads and saw a suited server holding a tray of delicate champagne flutes filled with liquid gold.

Liam grabbed two and handed one to me.

"So what's the fundraiser for?" I took a tiny sip of the champagne, staying in character. It was delicious.

"The Wounded Warrior charity. To support wounded veterans and their families."

I looked at everyone in their finery, at the incredible location, with their designer clothes draping everybody's bodies.

"They don't see the irony of raising money for veterans while showing off their gazillions in their fancy clothes?"

"I highly doubt it."

I met his gaze, remembering something I'd noted in my research on him. "Most of the charities you support help veterans."

He inclined his head. "Zane supports kids' charities. His father abandoned him and his mother when he was young. Mav's quiet about it, but he donates millions to charities that support education for kids, especially in science and technology. Rivera Tech supplies computers to hundreds of thousands of schools."

I gripped the stem of my wineglass. "Why veterans' charities for you?"

"Because they need help, they've more than earned it, and I'm in a position to help." He shrugged a shoulder. "I wanted to join the British Army after college. My father scuttled the idea after a few calls to certain generals."

"I'm sorry."

"All in the past now."

I knew better than anyone that past hurts were never gone. They dulled off, but managed to stab you when you least expected it.

He held out his arm.

I slipped mine through his.

I studied the crowd idly. I'd long ago perfected looking like I was taking no notice, but I was really cataloging everyone. Stopping by the food tables, I ignored the tiny, weird-looking canapes, and zeroed in on a tray full of truffles. I barely stifled a moan. Discreetly, I snagged two of the little balls.

"You like chocolate?"

I glanced at Liam and saw him smiling. I popped a truffle in my mouth, closed my eyes, and this time I did moan. It was *so* good.

When I opened my eyes, he was watching me with a look filled with heat. My belly filled with flutters. "Everyone likes chocolate."

"Not as much as you do."

I turned away, dragging in a breath, and ate the other truffle. I recognized a face and my insides froze.

Calmly, I turned back to face Liam. I cupped his cheek and pulled his head down to mine.

"Nexus is here," I murmured.

"What?" Keeping in character, he tucked my hair back behind my ear.

"I recognize the woman who delivered the blackmail note to me. Dyed-black hair, black dress."

"Shit."

"We can't slip up. We're a couple in lust. Let's do the rounds and then get out of here."

His hand slid lower, resting at the top of my ass. I fought back a shiver.

"That won't be hard," he said. "Come on."

He pulled me through the crowd. He nodded and smiled at people.

He was good at this. I kept my smile pinned in place and ignored all the speculative looks.

Don't worry, single society ladies, this billionaire isn't really mine.

No, billionaires didn't end up with workaholic private investigators.

"Would you like to dance, darling?" Liam drawled.

"Hell, no," I whispered. It was not an exaggeration to say that I had two left feet.

His hand squeezed my hip.

"Why, I'd love to," I gritted out.

He pulled me onto the dance floor. Thankfully, the music was slow.

Liam pulled me into his arms and I took a second to wonder that we fit so well together. Then I stepped on his foot.

He bravely hid his wince.

"I warned you," I whispered.

I felt the flex of his muscles, he had a long, lean body like a swimmer.

"Just let me lead," he murmured.

He glided across the dance floor, and I stumbled, and almost stepped on his foot again.

"I said let me lead, you're still trying to take over."

I frowned. "I'm used to being in charge."

"Relax."

"I'm pretty crap at that."

"I would never have guessed." He nuzzled the side of my head. "Trust me."

He moved me easily across the dance floor, and once I realized that I wasn't going to trip, I relaxed a little.

"You don't relax easily, do you?" Liam's mouth brushed my ear.

My hormones started tap-dancing through my system. The man was too potent. Too hot. Too everything.

As he moved against me, I indulged the desire running through me. It only took seconds for me to forget where I was, why I was there.

There was only Liam.

His gaze locked on mine. He didn't look away.

Suddenly, I realized the song had ended, we were still swaying against each other to our own song.

"Aspen." He cupped my cheeks, thumbs on my cheekbones.

Then he stiffened. I saw his face close down, and a flash of something dark in his eyes.

"Liam, what's wrong?" A part of me wanted to wrap my arms around him, comfort him. Take away that pain I'd seen in his eyes.

His jaw worked. "My father's headed this way."

Crap. "Your father's in New York?"

"Yes. He's in town, and I've declined to meet with him."

"Okay." I clung to Liam's arm as he hustled me off the dance floor.

"He wants to introduce me to his new fiancée." A pause. "Who's far younger than I am."

Well, Rupert Kensington was a real winner. "How long have they been engaged?"

"No clue, and I don't care. He's conveniently ignored the fact that he's still married to his last wife."

I wondered if this engagement had come before or after those ugly photos. "So his divorce isn't final?"

Liam shook his head.

"Liam," a deep voice drawled.

We turned. I slid an arm around Liam's lean waist. He wrapped his arm around my shoulders.

"Father." His tone was sharp and clipped.

Well, if I ever wanted to guess what Liam would look like as he aged, I now had the answer. Rupert Kensington looked like an older version of his son. Long, trim body, handsome face, and gold hair now smudged with distinguished gray at his temples.

The woman standing beside him smiled, her head tilted at an angle that looked painful. Her chestnut-brown hair was piled on her head in a complicated design. Her gaze was locked on Liam.

"It's so wonderful to run into you here." Rupert grinned, ignoring the tension. "Now you can meet Cressida."

"A pleasure," the young woman breathed.

Liam didn't even look at her, just nodded.

"And who is this delectable creature?" Rupert's gaze fell on me. His eyes were brown, not Liam's blue.

"Penn, this is my father and his fiancée." Liam's tone was colder than the polar ice cap.

"Hi," I said.

"My son follows in my footsteps. He has an eye for the beautiful ladies."

Liam stiffened, his fingers clenching on my hip. Cressida's laugh was like a small tinkle.

I covered Liam's hand with mine.

"Oh?" I cocked my head, then looked at Liam. "I thought you were estranged from your father, and that he was a massive asshole? I wouldn't have thought you followed in his footsteps. *At all.*"

Rupert's face froze. The good-natured look leached from his face, replaced by acid.

Cressida looked around, uncertain.

Liam's body relaxed, and then he laughed—a sexy, low laugh.

God, I really liked the sound of it.

"I like a woman with intelligence, Father, not just beauty. I like more than just arm candy. And I also like a woman who's an adult."

I heard the hidden message.

Anger flared on Rupert's face.

"We were just leaving." Liam tugged me away. "Enjoy the party, Father. Cressida."

Liam didn't stop until he'd towed me out of the ballroom.

Then he yanked me up, our mouths a whisper apart.

"I want to take you home and fuck you all night."

My body lit up. "Because of the dress, or because I mouthed off to your douchebag father?"

"Both. I like the whole package."

I sighed. It almost hurt to wrestle my desire into some sort of submission.

"Sorry. You're going back to your multi-million-dollar pad, and I'm going back to my apartment. Alone. Well, with my two sisters."

I'd also be going home hugely turned on to my empty bed.

"So strict," he murmured.

"We've criminals to bring down, remember?"

He tucked my hair back, setting my earring swinging. "I'm good at multitasking."

"Turn off the charm and sex appeal, Kensington. I can't handle much more of it."

He smiled. "You think I'm sexy?"

"You don't need me feeding your ego." The elevator arrived. "I'll see you tomorrow. We have a warehouse to search."

10

THEY'RE PROTECTIVE

Liam

L iam sat in the passenger seat of a plain, boring white Chevy sedan. Aspen sat behind the wheel.

Everyone believed they were holed up in his office for a meeting. But they'd snuck out and taken Aspen's vehicle.

"This is a crap car."

She arched a brow. "Sorry, I left my Aston at home."

He grunted. "It's still crap."

"Man, you are a snob. We're trying to blend in, remember?"

They were heading into the Bronx toward the warehouse. He tapped his fingers on the dash. He'd hoped to have heard something from Vander this morning, but all he had was a short text telling him they were still working on it.

"Have you been to the warehouse before?" she asked.

"No." Soon she turned onto the street where the

warehouse was, and Liam leaned forward. "That's it there."

They drove past the brick building. It was a solid block of red brick, several stories high at the front, and with a long, single story section at the back with large roller doors and a crumbling roof.

Aspen found a parking spot on the next street and they walked back.

Liam took out a key, and opened a large metal door at the front. It groaned as he pushed it open.

They stepped into the shadowed space. Pigeons took flight, casting flickering shadows in the light that filtered in through the grimy windows and single hole in the ceiling.

The place was filthy. There were puddles on the ground, piles of trash, and the scent of... He wasn't exactly sure what it was.

Aspen eyed his shoes and suit, a smile on her face. "Watch those shiny Italian shoes."

He noted that she'd worn navy-blue trousers and wedge heels today. She had a pretty blue shirt on, and a fitted jacket over the top.

They walked deeper into the space. Solid pillars marched in rows. There was some charming, creative graffiti on the wall. Liam wasn't sure that what the artist suggested was anatomically possible.

The remnants of a fire sat in the middle of the floor. Discarded drug paraphernalia lay around it.

"There's nothing here," she said.

They continued through the cavernous space. It was empty.

"Let's check upstairs," he said.

They navigated the rotten stairs. They found more graffiti, trash, and a whole lot of nothing. Frowning, Liam led her back downstairs. He pointed to a large, crumbling doorway.

"There's an adjoining part over here. It would have been the old loading docks."

The other section of the warehouse was darker. He heard things scuttling around in the shadows.

"We're missing something," she said.

Liam scanned the darkness. "I can't think what."

Suddenly, there was a noise out in the main part of the warehouse.

Aspen cursed and grabbed his arm.

They both pressed their backs to the brick wall.

Liam heard an echo of voices, and a second later, he heard the tinny sound of music.

He peered around the doorway.

"Who is it?" she whispered.

"I can't see. I'm going to take a look."

"No, wait—"

He slid through the doorway. He used some of the pillars for cover and got close to the sounds.

He spotted several teenagers sitting around. One was holding a phone that was playing music.

Liam stepped out from behind a pillar. "What are you doing here?"

There were curses, and the kids all jerked and stood. One kid almost tripped over his own feet.

An older boy—tall with broad shoulders—stepped forward. "Who the fuck are you?"

"The owner of this place."

"Fuck," a girl with pink hair muttered.

"We ain't stealing," the tall boy said.

Liam studied them. They all wore ragged clothes, and he noted several plastic bags nearby, loaded with stuff.

"You're staying here?"

A smaller boy lifted his head, chin jutting at Liam. "We stay wherever we want."

They were homeless. Probably runaways.

No doubt they all had hard stories to share. He gritted his teeth. "Well, I don't mind if you stay here. I'm just looking around."

The kids didn't relax, just watched him with gazes that were far too old.

"Here." He yanked out his wallet and grabbed some cash. "Get some pizza or something."

He held his hand out. The kids all blinked, eyeing him suspiciously.

Then a dark-skinned girl darted forward and snatched the money.

"That your woman?" the tall boy asked, with a nod of his head.

Liam turned his head and spotted Aspen in the shadows.

"Yes." Liam lowered his voice. "Although, she's not entirely on board with it yet, but I'm working on it.

The girl with the pink hair smiled. "She's crazy."

Liam smiled back. "We'll finish looking around, then go. Be careful."

He turned.

"Hey..."

Liam turned back to see the tall boy watching him. Liam raised a brow.

"There have been some dudes here. At night. Late at night."

Pink Hair girl nodded. "They have flashlights, but they're sneaky. They don't want people to see them."

Liam frowned. "Thanks. Make sure you stay clear of them."

He walked over to Aspen.

"That wad of hundreds will buy a lot of pizza," she noted.

He shrugged.

"Never pegged you for a soft touch, Liam." Her lips quirked. "Good to see you're a nice guy under the money."

"No man wants to hear that he's a nice guy, Aspen. We want to be tough, rugged, and masculine."

"Come on, Mr. Nice Guy. There's something you need to see."

She led him back into the other section of the warehouse that lay in darkness. She pulled out a flashlight, and they followed the narrow beam of light along the wall.

She flipped it upward.

Liam frowned. Bricks had been knocked out of the wall. There were holes dotted all through the long expanse of brick.

He crouched and studied some of the bricks. "It appears as if someone was looking for something."

"I agree." She touched the wall. "This looks like the oldest part of the warehouse. The front part is newer."

Liam spotted some paper on the ground and picked it up. It was old, yellow, and brittle.

It looked like some sort of label. He pocketed it. It was probably just trash, but he'd check it later. "What the hell would someone be looking for in here?"

Noises echoed from the main warehouse again. But this time, there were deeper voices, and the music cut off.

"Get out of here!" a man yelled.

"Fuck you, asshole." That was the tall kid's voice.

"Turn the light off," Liam said.

Aspen flicked the switch. They were plunged into darkness.

Liam took her hand, and they moved along the wall.

"This way," a voice called out.

Liam heard footsteps.

"They're coming this way," Aspen whispered.

It had to be Nexus, but Liam had no way to know for sure.

"We need to get out," he said.

"Is there a back way?"

"No idea."

The people were getting closer. Liam saw beams of light.

"Come on," he said.

They hurried through the darkness. He stepped in a puddle, and felt water seep into his shoes. He muttered a curse.

They reached the back wall.

"I want you to see this," a man's voice said.

The lights were cutting through the darkness, moving closer toward Aspen and Liam.

"Down." Aspen hit him and they dropped to the dirty floor. "Shh." She pressed a hand over his mouth.

He stayed still, with her body pressed against his.

A light shone on the wall above their heads.

"And over here." The lights moved away.

"Crawl," she whispered.

They crawled along the dirty floor. This was *not* how Liam had planned to spend his day.

The voices got quieter.

"Look." She nudged him.

He saw the rectangle of light set in the wall. It was the outline around an old metal door.

"Let's go." He rose and opened the door, then dragged her outside.

They jogged down the street and turned. More old warehouses lined the streets.

No one followed them.

"Thank God." She stopped and looked at him. Then she snort-laughed. "You're filthy."

Liam glanced down and saw that his hands were black, his white shirt was smeared with grime, and he'd probably have to throw his suit out.

Damn it. It was a bespoke Gieves & Hawkes.

Aspen hadn't fared much better. She had black smears on her cheeks, and her clothes were dirty. Her jacket was stained with...well, he wasn't quite sure what it was.

"We can't go back to the office like this," he said. "We'll stop by my place and clean up."

Aspen

I stood in the huge shower, the size of my entire bathroom, and washed my hair.

I seriously coveted this bathroom. Liam had given me his master bath, and said that he'd shower in a guest room. The guy had four other bathrooms to choose from.

Desperately, I was trying *not* to think about the fact that Liam stood in this very spot every day, naked, with water cascading over him.

Heat curled in my belly.

With a groan, I dumped my head under the water.

Think about Nexus, Aspen. Think about poor Jake.

My thoughts turned to the Bronx warehouse.

What the hell were they after in that place? The place was a dirty, crumbling mess. There was nothing inside of it. Why the hell were they poking holes in the walls?

All I had were lots of questions, and no answers. I climbed out of the shower and dried off with a huge, fluffy towel. I'd sponged the worst of the dirt off my slacks, but my shirt and jacket were write offs.

In my bra and panties, I toweled my hair dry, then bundled it up damp on my head.

I needed to borrow a shirt.

When I stepped into Liam's glorious bedroom, I paused.

It was so nice. The huge bed was covered with a soft, gray comforter and lots of pillows. A rich-looking, cream rug was centered under the bed. I'd put a tall plant in the corner. Some smaller ones on the dresser.

Quit redecorating the man's bedroom. I saw a white button up shirt laid out on the bed and smiled.

I pulled it on and moaned. So soft. I was going to steal it. I buttoned it up, and my gaze snagged once again on the view of the city.

"Hey, are you decent?" Liam appeared in the doorway.

I spun. His gaze flared, seeing me in his shirt, then slowly drifted down my bare legs.

Lots of places blazed to life inside me. I cleared my throat. "You haven't showered yet?"

He was still in his ruined shirt, tie, and trousers.

"I got a call from the office." He cocked his head. "What are you wearing under that?"

I rolled my eyes. "None of your business."

He grinned. He was so damn handsome. No one had the right to be so gorgeous. It was unfair to us mere mortals.

"It's nearly lunch time. Why don't you see what I have in the kitchen for us to eat before we head back to the office?"

"Sure." I could manage a sandwich without poisoning our taste buds.

But Liam still didn't move. "I really like you in my shirt, Aspen."

"Fair warning, I'm stealing it."

He crossed the room, and suddenly I got the feeling like a predator had entered my space.

"Keep your distance, Kensington." Wow, that sounded really unconvincing.

He stopped, just inches between us. My hands itched to touch him. To rip those clothes off and drag him to the floor.

"I'll stay right here," he said. "Think you can keep your hands off me?"

"I don't know how you walk around with that big head all day."

"Walk right past me, Aspen, without touching me."

I lifted my chin and strode to him. Then I grabbed his tie and yanked his head down.

The kiss was hard and hungry. Desire was a wicked rush inside me, and I pulled in the taste of him.

Then I broke the kiss and leaned back, licking my lips.

He was grinning.

"I kept my hands off you," I said. "I touched your tie. And lips don't count."

He laughed, and I strode out smiling. My slacks needed a bit more time to dry, so I left them tossed over a chair.

I figured Liam had already gotten a good look at my bare legs.

I opened the enormous refrigerator. Briar and Juno loved to cook, and they'd squee all over this fancy kitchen and its expensive appliances.

I pulled out some meats and cheeses. I was thinking about making sandwiches, but the fancy prosciutto, brie, and—I squinted at another frou-frou cheese. I had no idea what it was, but it had blue bits in it. I didn't do moldy cheese. These weren't really the right fixings for humble sandwiches.

I heard a beep, and the front door opened.

Oh, hell. I froze.

Two tall men sauntered in and I recognized them instantly.

Not many people in New York wouldn't recognize Zane Roth and Maverick Rivera.

They spotted me and stopped like they'd hit a wall. Zane Roth was the perfect definition of tall, dark, and handsome. A frown crossed his attractive face.

"What the fuck?" Maverick clipped out. "What the ever-loving fuck?"

Maverick Rivera wasn't handsome. He was too rough and rugged to be called anything as tame as handsome. He was a few inches taller than Zane, and his shoulders were broader. He looked like he should be a bouncer at a club, not a billionaire.

I'd seen a bad winter storm roll in over New York once. Rivera's face looked like that.

I guessed that Liam had mentioned the whole blackmail thing to his friends at some stage.

"Penn Channing," Zane said.

I stepped out from behind the island. "Um—"

Instantly, they took in my bare legs, Liam's shirt, my wet hair, and my makeup-free face.

Both men's faces darkened. I held out a hand. "It's not what it looks like."

I winced. *Oh, that was really lame.*

"What are you doing here?" Zane asked.

"Who gives a fuck?" Maverick pulled out his phone. "I'm calling the police."

"Don't." Shit, where was Liam? "Look—"

"Hey, have you made some food? Our activities this morning have me starved." Liam waltzed in, wearing new suit pants, and a fresh shirt that was still unbuttoned.

Oh. *Hell.*

This all looked and sounded really bad.

He jerked to a halt, looking at his friends. "What are you two doing here?"

"Well, we heard you were very cozy with a redhead last night at the fundraiser," Zane said. "Then we stopped by your office, only for Eleanor to inform us that you were *out*, and lunching at home. So, we stopped by."

Maverick crossed his muscular arms over his chest. "We didn't expect to find you fucking your blackmailer."

I winced. Maverick Rivera had one hell of a temper. "I told them that it isn't what it looks like."

Liam made a face. "I bet that helped."

I leaned against the island and gave him a small shake of my head. We couldn't reveal the details of what we were doing to these men. The more people who knew, the greater the chance of it getting back to Doyle and Nexus.

Liam nodded and sighed. "I need you guys to trust me. I know what I'm doing."

Zane was watching us intently, something working in his eyes.

"No!" Maverick snapped. "You're one of my best friends. I'm not going to let you get dragged under by some blackmailing, criminal bitch."

"I'm asking you to trust me, Mav. There are things I can't share yet."

Maverick cursed, his hands on his hips and his gaze dropping to his shoes.

"You sure?" Zane asked, his tone intense.

Liam nodded.

"If you need us, we're here."

Man, it must be nice to have friends like that. I had my sisters, and friends like Erica, who I had drinks with when we could make the time. I had informants, reluctant colleagues, and Jack, the retired PI who taught me everything I knew. But I didn't have friends like this.

"Thanks, Zane." Liam looked at Rivera. "Mav."

Liam shepherded the two billionaires out. Before he left, Maverick speared me with a look hot enough to scar.

"Sorry," Liam said. "They're protective."

"Don't be sorry. You're lucky to have friends like that."

His gaze was on me, like he was trying to see into my head. "So, what did you throw together for lunch?"

"Well, I took out some ham and cheese, and I arranged them on the counter. Then I put the moldy cheese back in the fridge."

"It's called pule. It's six hundred dollars a pound."

"*Really?*" Man, rich people bought strange things. "I don't care if it's worth more than diamonds." I waved a hand at the island. "And that's about the extent of my cooking skills."

"Don't cook?"

"Not if I can help it."

"Luckily, I do. I'll make dinner for us tonight."

"Liam—"

"So we can discuss Nexus, and why they want the warehouse. I'm hoping we hear from Vander today. He's going to send through what he can find."

I watched Liam. The man was a walking temptation. I needed to keep my guard up.

But he was right. We needed to work out what was going on with Nexus, and save Jake.

"All right. But dinner and work only."

"So strict, darling."

11

WOULD PANICKING HELP?

Liam

The salmon sizzled in the pan on the stove. Liam swiveled, stirring the simmering liquid in the other pot.

"That smells great."

He glanced over. Aspen sat on a stool at the island, a glass of Shiraz in front of her.

"Thanks. It's Alaskan Salmon with lemon-butter sauce."

"I never knew billionaires could cook."

"Us billionaires are full of surprises."

They'd headed back to the office for the afternoon, and he'd been inundated with work. Now, he wanted them to relax, and eat a meal.

But the threat of Nexus still loomed.

Liam thought of his mother, Annabelle, the kids. If those photos got out...

He sighed. Annabelle had left a voicemail for him.

She was excited because she was starting a new online business selling designer accessories—scarves, jewelry, belts, handbags. A way to support herself in the wake of the upcoming divorce.

His mother had also left a message. Going off about his father's very young, new fiancée.

If his father's scandal got splashed everywhere, it would tank Annabelle's new venture. It would also send his mother into a rage-filled breakdown.

Aspen swirled her wine, and Liam's gaze caught on the inked words on her forearm. "What's your tattoo say?"

"Oh." She lifted her arm. "All I can do is be me, whoever that is."

"Wise words."

"I got it when I graduated high school. I was at a bit of a crossroads, finding myself, and deciding what to do with my life."

Pretty astute for a teenager.

Her phone vibrated on the island. She looked at it, and tapped in a message. It buzzed again. Then again.

She made an annoyed noise. More tapping.

"Everything okay?" he asked.

"My sisters. Nineteen-year-old busybodies, who think the world revolves around them." Her lips twitched.

It was obvious she loved them.

Liam had grown up an only child until he'd been a teenager. Then he'd had a whole slew of half siblings. He didn't have a relationship with them like Aspen did. He felt more like an uncle. He was closest with Annabelle's kids. George and Amelia were great. George a little pistol, and Amelia was quiet, sweet, and always hugging the stuffed bear that Liam had given her.

He released a breath. He hated to think of what a sex scandal would do to them.

Aspen's phone rang and she snatched it up.

"I told you, I'll be home late. Don't wait up." A pause. "Out." Another pause. "I'm having dinner." Now an annoyed sigh. "None of your business, Juno." Aspen rolled her eyes. "How are you going to find out? I'm the PI in the family, remember?" She snorted. "I love you, too." She set the phone down and sipped her wine. "They're always in my business."

"Do they know about the investigation?" He got out some plates to serve the fish.

"They know I'm undercover, but not the details. They don't know I'm at Kensington Group. God, they'd lose their minds." She smiled. "Like most of the female population of New York, they lose their minds over the billionaire bachelors."

Liam started serving up the salmon. "But not you?"

"Takes more to impress me than a pretty face and several billion dollars."

Shaking his head in amusement, he carried dinner to the table. As they ate, Aspen's eyes closed several times as she savored the meal.

He smiled. He liked knowing she enjoyed his cooking.

"Who taught you to cook?" she asked.

"My family's personal chef. My parents traveled a lot, and if I wasn't in a boarding school, I was left with our staff. Henri was French, and an absolute snob, and pretended he hated teaching me. Secretly, I think he enjoyed it."

After they ate, they spread their files and papers on the coffee table. Liam grabbed his tablet, and made them coffee.

She opened her laptop—it was a couple of years old, and a little dinged. He noted that it was Rivera Tech brand.

She tapped in some searches. Made some frustrated noises. "Nothing of interest comes up on that warehouse. I can't work out why the hell Nexus wants it. I can run a search on all the companies that have owned or used it. But it'll take some time."

His gut cramped. "And we're running out of time."

She reached across and grabbed his hand. "We're not letting those photos go public. And we aren't letting Jake get hurt."

He nodded.

She squeezed then released his fingers, then tapped again on her laptop. Her brow furrowed. She was cute as hell when she concentrated.

His cell phone rang and he saw Vander's name on the screen. *Finally.* "It's Vander."

Aspen got a funny look on her face.

Liam frowned. "What?"

"Vander Norcross is a *legend.*" She shivered a little.

Liam's frown deepened. Did she have to look like a teenage fan at a boyband concert? He pressed the speaker button. "Vander."

"Hey, Liam. I have some intel for you." The man's deep voice filled the room.

"Good, because we're running out of time."

"First off, Penn Channing is an alias of a woman called Aspen Chandler."

Aspen pulled a face.

"I'm not sure how she fits into all this," Vander continued, "but she's a licensed investigator."

"I know," Liam said. "She's sitting here with me."

"Um, hi." Aspen's voice sounded a little breathy.

Liam nudged her. "Vander, let me bring you up to speed on things." He gave Vander a brief rundown on Aspen, Erica and Jake, the warehouse, the fact that Nexus was looking for something at the place.

Vander expelled a breath. "Okay, that complicates things a bit. Ace hasn't had anything pop on why these assholes want your warehouse, but we've dug up plenty on Nexus. The group is run by a guy called—"

"Kristoff Doyle," Aspen said. "Doesn't show his face and is very, very careful."

"Yeah," Vander said. "Guy keeps a very low profile, and we dug up zero on him. That concerns me. His second-in-command is a woman named Jackie Godin. Woman is bad news and has a string of white-collar crimes to her name, along with several charges for assault. She likes to cut, shoot, and beat people up."

"Charming," Liam said.

"Does she have badly dyed black hair and soulless eyes?" Aspen asked.

"That's her. Nexus has been in operation for over a

decade. Mostly corporate and insurance fraud, blackmail. I suspect Doyle's work goes back even earlier, he was just less organized then. They're really dangerous, Liam. They won't hesitate to kill in order to get what they want."

Liam felt the burn of rage. A huge helping of it was for his bastard of a father, but the rest was for Nexus. "Well, Nexus aren't getting this land. If I hand it over it would scuttle a massive, billion-dollar project set to provide vital housing for the area. No, I want Jake Knox back safely, those photos destroyed, and Nexus stopped. If I give in to their demands, they'll be back for more."

"Okay," Vander said. "Lay low. Ace is still searching for anything on the warehouse. We find out why they want it, it'll help us find a way to stop them."

"Thanks, Vander," Liam said.

"I'll be in touch."

The call ended. Aspen pushed her hair back and sighed. "We need to keep looking."

They got back to work. Liam rose and made coffee. He also pulled a small box out of his pantry.

He set it down beside Aspen.

She saw it and gasped. "Oh my God, is that from Jean-Paul Hévin?"

"Yes."

"He's like the best chocolatier in Paris!" She stared at the small chocolate squares in awe.

"All yours." Liam felt a flush of pleasure to give her something she liked.

She snatched one up, ate it, and sighed. "Oh, wow."

Now, if only he could get her to look at him the way she looked at that chocolate.

As Aspen savored another chocolate, Liam remembered the scrap of paper he'd picked up at the warehouse. He fished it out of his ruined suit and smoothed it out.

Aspen leaned over and frowned. "What's that?"

"I picked it up at the warehouse."

"It looks like a label."

Liam squinted. "I think it is. From a bottle." The ink was faded. "Look, I think that says whiskey."

"The old part of the warehouse is from Prohibition times, right? Could they have made bootlegged whiskey in there?"

"This isn't for whiskey, it's for beer. They might have brewed it there, or at least distributed it out of that warehouse back in the 1920s and 30s." He wasn't sure how that helped them.

She went back to her searches.

"How did you become a private investigator?" Liam asked.

"It started after my dad was arrested and went to jail. I got a part time job."

"You said you're still in contact with your father?"

"Sporadic. He moves around a lot. He's in Arizona at the moment, I think. He calls occasionally. Anyway, my mom divorced him. She had no useful skills, and she was having trouble coping. She's an artist, so she painted, but it wasn't enough to pay the rent and feed all four of us, so I got a job after school."

Liam stilled. "Wait. You were fourteen, adjusting to a new school, helping with young twins, and you got a job?"

She shrugged a shoulder. "I did what I had to do."

It sounded like Aspen Chandler didn't take after her mother or father. She didn't look for an easy way out or check out of a tough situation. No, she rolled up her sleeves and dived into hard work.

"I got a job filing for this crusty PI. Jack is a loner, grumpy, and difficult with a capital *D*." She smiled. "I loved it. I tidied and reorganized his office. It was a disaster. He lost his mind." She shook her head. "He didn't treat me with pity, or look at me with that ugly curiosity like others did who knew about my father. I learned everything I could in the office, then slowly, he started taking me on surveillance jobs, and sent me to do small tasks." She grinned. "I loved it. I'm good at it. He taught me everything I know. When I finished high school, there was no money for college, and I couldn't leave the twins."

He understood the words she'd had inked on her skin better now. "So you set up your own business."

"Not at first. I worked with Jack for a bit until I got my license. I have no regrets." She looked back at the papers and laptop. "Although I like it better when investigations go more smoothly than this."

"Where's Jack now?"

"He did the one thing I never expected, and retired." A sad look crossed her face. "He moved to Florida, and spends his days fishing. Sends me postcards, and calls, occasionally."

Her phone rang and she huffed out a breath. "Those girls are going to drive me crazy." She snatched up the phone, and paused. "It's my burner phone." Her face hardened. "Doyle."

Liam tensed and watched her rise. She thumbed a button.

"Doyle."

"How's it progressing with Kensington?"

Liam stiffened at the deep voice. It was accent-less, educated.

Who was this asshole?

"You gave me three days," Aspen said.

"And now you have two."

She met Liam's gaze. "I'll get what you want."

"Where are you now?"

She frowned. "At Kensington's. He cooked me a very nice dinner. Salmon with lemon-butter sauce. I've just finished fucking him and he's in the shower. He likes it when I'm on top, and has a very energetic cock. Anything else you'd like to know?"

Despite the seriousness, Liam felt a spurt of amusement. He grinned, and her lips twitched.

He also felt a shot of gut-deep desire.

He wanted Aspen riding him, or under him, he didn't care what position, as long as his cock was lodged deep inside her.

"Get me that deed, Penn." Doyle ended the call.

Aspen blew out a breath. "He's losing patience."

"I don't give a fuck."

"It makes him even more dangerous." She closed her laptop. "I'd better get home."

He strode to her. "You should stay."

"The twins. And I told you, we can't afford the distraction. If I stay, we both know we won't be sleeping."

Anger and frustration swirled in Liam. "Is it so easy

for you to turn off? Are you so used to being undercover that pretending is easy for you?"

He saw the flash of hurt before she hid it.

Liam mentally cursed himself.

"I need to go." She stuffed her things in her bag.

"I'll drive you."

She looked up. "It's not easy. You're not a man who's easy to ignore."

"Aspen—"

"Liam, I'm trying to be realistic here. You're a billionaire, from a wealthy family. I'm a PI, and not from a wealthy anything. We are nothing alike."

"Bollocks," he snapped.

"You're out of my league."

"There are no leagues, Aspen. I'm a man, you're a woman. How much money we have doesn't dictate who we are." He leaned closer. "Or how we'd be together."

Surprising him, she grabbed him, and then her mouth was on his.

The kiss was hot, a little frantic. She slid a hand into his hair, he cupped her ass. His groan vibrated through his chest.

When she pulled back, they were both panting.

"We need to go now." Her voice was husky.

"When this is over, Aspen..." He flexed his hand.

"We'll see." She slid her bag over her shoulder.

"No, not we'll see. You'll be in my bed."

She tossed her hair back. "That's my choice, Kensington."

He followed her to the elevator. Damned if her attitude didn't turn him on more.

They didn't talk on the drive to her place.

It started raining, and the only sound was the swish of the windshield wipers.

They stopped at a traffic light. The light turned green, and Liam accelerated.

"Watch out!" Aspen screamed.

A large black SUV ran the red light, speeding through the intersection, rushing straight at them.

Liam slammed on the brakes. The Aston's tires slid on the wet road, and the car spun.

He heard Aspen gasp. The SUV was right in front of them.

The Aston jerked to a stop.

"Fuck." He squeezed the wheel. Rain pattered hard on the windshield.

The SUV had stopped too, just inches away.

Then suddenly, the doors of the Aston were wrenched open.

Hooded figures appeared, grabbing at them.

With a cry, Aspen was yanked out.

"Come quietly, and we won't kill the woman." A man loomed over Liam, pistol in hand.

Fuck. Liam slid out of the car.

"Let me go." Aspen struggled, trying to break free of her captor. The man punched her in the back of her head, and she slumped.

Liam gritted his teeth to keep himself from attacking the bastard.

"Move it," the other man said.

Be okay, Aspen.

Aspen

I blinked awake. My head throbbed, and I was lying in darkness.

Where was I?

"You okay?"

Liam's deep voice. I felt him shift against me and realized he was pressed up against my back.

We were lying in... I squinted, feeling vibration under me.

In the trunk of a car.

"Oh, shit," I muttered.

"An apt pronouncement."

"How can you sound so calm? We've been kidnapped!"

"Would panicking help?"

How dare he sound so amused? God, I'd been kidnapped and locked in the trunk of a moving vehicle with a billionaire.

Not how I imagined my evening would end.

I tried to move and heard the clank of metal. I registered the cool band around my left wrist.

"Oh my God, they handcuffed us together?"

Liam moved his arm and the handcuffs jangled.

"What the hell does Doyle think he's doing?" I snapped.

"Intimidating me."

Liam didn't sound intimidated. He sounded annoyed, with a side of angry.

"I'm busy plotting how the hell to make my father pay. This is all his fucking fault."

I wasn't going anywhere near that. "What do we do now?" I felt around. The trunk was empty except for Liam's hard body curled around me.

"We wait until they stop."

I made a sound. I didn't want to wait. The twins would be worried.

"You aren't jumping from a moving vehicle, Aspen."

Damn, he was probably right.

The car drove for what felt like forever. Meanwhile, it was extremely distracting to have Liam spooning me.

Finally, the car slowed.

I tensed. The trunk opened.

It was dark, but I saw the two hooded figures just fine. They dragged us out of the trunk, and that's when I realized that I didn't have on any shoes. Liam didn't, either.

"Who are you?" I demanded.

My answer was another shove.

I collided with Liam, and he pulled me closer.

"Move." One of our captors gestured.

I saw the hulking shadow of a building looming over us, and heard the lap of waves. We were near the water somewhere.

One of the goons opened a rusty roller door and we were shoved into a warehouse.

A light clicked on. A lone bulb hung down over two wooden chairs.

Still handcuffed, Liam and I were shoved into the chairs. Goon One started tying my uncuffed right wrist to the arm of the chair with some rope. I glanced over and saw Goon Two doing the same to Liam.

"What happens now?" I demanded. "What do you want?"

They ignored me and walked out.

"Well," Liam said.

I dragged in a breath. I was sitting in a cavernous empty warehouse, tied to a chair, and shackled to a billionaire bachelor. I had no shoes. No phone. No money.

Don't panic, Aspen.

"This has to be Doyle," I said.

"That's my guess." Liam tugged on his tied arm.

"Well, I'm not going to fucking sit here." I bucked and yanked on the rope, but it didn't budge. The handcuffs rattled.

"My rope has a little slack," he said.

I peered over, but it was hard to see. The bulb didn't give off much light. "Can you work it free?"

"I'll try my best." He made a noise. "I can't get my fingers to it."

I sucked in a breath. "I'll try."

"How?"

I stood, lifting my entire chair with me. "Hold still." I leaned over him, the handcuffs making it hard. It was awkward as hell. I was half draped over his lap, the wooden chair pressed against my back, one arm handcuffed to him, and my other wrist hurt from the rope.

I got my teeth on Liam's rope. *Yuk.*

Trying not to think about the germs, I tried to work the rope free with my teeth.

He made a sound and I looked up. "What's wrong?"

"Nothing." He was staring above my head.

"What?" I repeated.

"Well, you're lying over my lap..."

That's when I felt the growing bulge beneath me. "We've been kidnapped, and tied up, and you're getting turned on?"

"Trying not to. Just focus on the rope."

Right. It was much harder to focus when I could feel his hard cock against my belly.

Shit, now *I* was turned on.

I gave a hard yank with my teeth, and his rope came free.

"Yes!" I tried to get back up, but was pinned by my damn chair.

"Hang on." Liam gave me a push.

My chair hit the concrete, and I dropped back into it. Liam rose, shaking his free arm while our other wrists were still handcuffed together.

"You next," he said.

We might still be handcuffed to each other, but once I was free of the chair, we could at least get out of here.

Liam knelt in front of me. He leaned over me as he worked on the rope, one handed.

"The bastard did this up tight."

I heard a noise. The screech of rusty metal.

There was a door opening somewhere. The sound echoed through the warehouse.

"Someone's coming," I hissed.

Liam rose. "Come on." He lifted my chair off the ground.

We awkwardly hobbled across the warehouse.

Oh, God. I was handcuffed to Liam, and tied to a chair, and trying to make a run for it. Jack would die laughing.

We passed through a doorway.

"Look," Liam said.

I saw the shadow of a forklift, and some tools and workbenches set up in the corner. It looked like some sort of workshop.

Liam rummaged through the tools, and lifted a knife.

I stilled. "If you cut me..."

"Trust me." His teeth were white in the darkness.

I didn't have a choice, but I suddenly realized that over the last two days, Liam Kensington had earned my trust.

"Do it."

He sawed through the rope, and a second later I was free of the chair.

That's when I heard shouts echo through the warehouse.

"We need to go," he said. "*Now.*"

We ran together, trying to find some sort of rhythm with our cuffed hands. We found a wall and moved along it. I stepped on something with my bare foot and winced.

No time to worry about it.

"Here." Liam stopped in front of a door.

He opened the lock, then shoved the door open.

It made a huge groan.

"Fuck." Liam gripped my fingers. "Run!"

The cold night air hit us as we sprinted down a row

of huge warehouses. Shouts echoed through the night behind us.

I had no clue exactly where we were, but the water was to our right. We reached the end, and I realized we had nowhere to go. We had warehouses to the left, water to the right, and water ahead of us.

Cursing, Liam tried the door to the closest warehouse. "Locked."

I saw flashlight beams bouncing as people were running toward us. They were coming.

We both faced the water.

The water would be cold. Very cold.

Oh. *God*.

His gaze met mine. "No other option."

I nodded and we walked to the edge. "On three."

"Okay," he said.

"One. Two—"

He jumped, pulling me with him.

12

DON'T CRASH, KENSINGTON

Liam

They hit the water with a splash.

Damn, it was cold.

Aspen came up sputtering.

"Shh," Liam warned. "Take it easy."

It was not easy to swim while handcuffed together. Shouts and flashlights sounded from the shoreline. He saw shadowy figures by the warehouse, flashlight beams arcing through the night.

"That way." Liam pointed.

She nodded, and they moved through the water, finding a rhythm.

They swam farther away from the warehouse. The water stank. He was going to have to sacrifice another suit. It was also freezing. They needed to get out and fast.

"There," Aspen said.

They were out of view of their captors now. Another warehouse was perched by the edge of the water. It was dark, and there was no sign of anyone around.

They pulled themselves out onto the dirt, and then stumbled up onto the concrete.

Aspen started shivering, her teeth chattering.

"How the hell...w-will we get out of h-here?" she asked. "We've got no phones. No m-money."

"Come here." He pulled her up and hugged her. "We'll sort it out."

She shivered harder and clung to him, burrowing closer.

"I-I need a hot shower and a shot of w-whiskey."

"I have a shower and a bottle of Macallan. You like Macallan?"

She snorted. "Sure. I have expensive bottles of Scotch lying around all the time."

"Come on, Chandler. Let's move."

A chain-link fence lay ahead of them, separating the warehouse from the street. Liam was pondering how best to climb it, when a low growl echoed behind them.

Bloody hell. He stiffened and scanned the darkness.

"Oh, shit," Aspen muttered. A black dog appeared. A rottweiler.

It was inside the fence with them.

And it had very sharp teeth.

It growled again, its gaze locked on them.

Liam and Aspen backed up.

"Nice doggy," Aspen said. "Move slowly."

Liam tried to stay calm.

"Liam? You okay?"

"I don't like dogs."

"I'm not fond of them myself."

"Especially not slavering Rottweilers, keen to maul us, and tear our hearts out."

She stared at him. "Jeez, did you have a bad experience as a kid?"

"As a matter of fact, yes. With my mother's poodle."

He heard a snicker.

"They have fangs too," he told her.

"Right." She sounded like she was barely suppressing a laugh.

The rottweiler snarled.

Shit. Liam's back hit the fence.

"On three, we'll spin and climb," she said.

The dog snarled again.

"Okay, screw the countdown," she said. "Go!"

They spun and jumped. The dog leaped and Liam heard it hit the fence. He climbed fast. He and Aspen worked their way to the top. Trying to figure out how to get over the top, while handcuffed, was tricky.

"Careful," she warned.

Liam got his leg over, and started down the other side. The metal cuff dug into his wrist. Aspen was right at the top, maneuvering.

Then Liam's foot slipped. *Shit.*

He fell, his fingers losing their grip on the chain link. Cursing, he turned.

He heard Aspen cry out as his weight pulled her off the fence.

His back hit the ground on the other side of the fence with a *thump.*

And Aspen landed on top of him.

He found himself with a very nice pair of breasts pressed to his face.

"Oh. *God*." She tried to push herself up, then slipped on top of him again. "I'm so sorry."

A laugh welled in his chest.

She cursed and slid to the side.

"I'm fine," he said. "Take your time."

"Are you laughing, Kensington?"

A small chuckle escaped him. "No."

"Liam!"

"I can think of worse things than your lovely breasts in my face."

She tried to push up again, and Liam sat up, helping her.

She stared at him, then started laughing too.

Behind the fence, the rottweiler barked at them.

"Oh, God." Still laughing, she leaned forward and kissed Liam.

Mmm. Laughing and kissing wasn't a combination he'd tried before.

He drank her in. He liked it, liked her. Too much.

"We'd better find a way out of here," she said.

They helped each other up, and got to the street. The dog continued to bark, and he hoped it didn't alert their kidnappers.

"What if our captors are out there, looking for us?" she asked. "What if we flag down the wrong person?"

"Let's put some distance between us and them."

They stuck to the shadows. They were in an industrial area and there was no one around.

As they crossed the street, he saw some homeless people sitting in the darkness, watching them carefully.

"We're in New York City, there should be someone around with a freaking phone," she said.

They turned down another street.

If they could get to a phone, he could call for help.

A moment later, he heard the drone of an engine.

A motorcycle came into view. The guy wasn't going very fast and didn't look like he was actively looking for anyone. Liam decided to take a risk. He stepped onto the road and waved with his uncuffed hand.

The motorcycle slowed to a stop and a young man pushed up the visor of his helmet.

"You guys okay?" He eyed their bare feet.

"Actually, we're not," Liam said.

The man looked at their handcuffed wrists, their disheveled, wet clothes, then looked up.

His eyes widened. "Holy shit, you're... Are you really...?"

"I am," Liam said. "I don't have my wallet on me, but I *really* need your bike. I'll give you double what it's worth."

Aspen made a choked sound.

"I'll give you my phone number, and you can call me tomorrow, and I'll pay you." Liam smiled. "I'm good for it."

The younger man stared at him, his mouth hanging open.

"Do we have a deal?" Liam asked.

"Hell, yeah."

The man scrambled off his bike.

"What's your name?"

"Harry."

"I'll give you my private number, Harry." Liam rattled off the digits and Harry yanked a scrap of paper and pen from his pocket.

"No one will believe this," Harry breathed.

"Will you be okay?" Liam asked.

"Yeah, I live around the corner above my father's shop. Man, I have a *billionaire's* number."

With a salute, Harry jogged off into the night.

"He'll probably sell you out to the tabloids," Aspen said.

"There's my cynical private investigator."

She eyed the bike dubiously. "So, can you operate a motorcycle?"

"I'm sure it isn't hard." He swung his leg over the bike and checked the controls.

Her gaze narrowed. "You look pretty comfy there."

He grinned at her. "I was just kidding. Mav, Zane, and I have taken some bike trips." He gunned the bike's engine. "Climb on."

She edged closer. "How?"

Crap, the whole handcuff situation made it tough. "You'll have to sit in front of me, facing me."

Aspen looked up at the sky. With a shake of her head, she managed to get on the bike in front of him. She plastered herself against him and wrapped her free arm around him.

"The things I do for my work," she muttered. "Don't crash, Kensington."

"Trust me, Ms. Chandler."

He took off.

She gripped him tighter and he felt her shiver.

Time to get out of here, and get her safe.

Aspen

I was officially a block of ice.

Even the warmth of Liam's body couldn't fend off the giant shivers racking my body. He patted my thigh.

I glanced around the streets and noted that we were almost at his place. We whizzed down Fifth Avenue. We must look like crazy people. Some cars honked at us.

The aches in my body were making themselves known. My wrist stung, my feet were sore, but the cold was the worst.

We turned, approaching his building, and I saw the cars out front, and lights from police cars.

Oh, shit.

Liam pulled the bike to a stop. The small crowd turned to stare at us.

We were a mess. Wet, barefoot, and on a motorbike with our chests pressed together.

Zane and Mav pulled away from the crowd.

"Jesus, Liam, are you okay?" Zane flicked a glance at me, then back to his friend.

"We're okay," Liam said.

Mav looked like a volcano about to erupt.

An attractive, black-haired woman touched Zane's arm and he pulled her close.

"We were worried, Liam," the woman said.

"The police found your Aston in the middle of the road, open, abandoned," Mav said.

"Witnesses said you and a woman were dragged away by masked men," Zane added.

Liam helped me off the bike and then he slid off. Our handcuffs clanked and everyone stared.

A police officer cleared his throat. "Mr. Kensington, if you're okay, I'll cancel the citywide search for you."

"Thank you, Officer," Liam said.

"The Aston's in your garage," Zane said.

"And this must be yours."

I looked up to see the dark-haired woman holding out my bag.

"Thanks." I took it.

The woman smiled. "I'm Monroe."

I nodded. I'd read the stories about her—she was the owner of a locksmith store, and daughter of a thief. She was also the woman who'd captured the heart of Zane Roth.

Fishing around in my bag, I sighed with relief when I found my personal phone. I pulled the device out, and glanced over at Liam. He was talking to the police.

I saw several missed calls from my sisters, and my belly clenched. I dialed.

"My God, I was so worried," Juno said.

"I know. Sorry. Something came up. I'm okay, Juno."

There were murmurs. "Aspen!" Briar came on the line. "We were about to call the *police*."

"Briar, I'm fine. Look, I don't know when I'll be back. But I'm safe, I promise."

"What's going on?" My sister's voice changed. "My God, are you with a guy?"

Mav, Monroe, and Zane were watching me. I turned slightly away. "It's work-related."

"It's a guy! Juno, she's with a guy."

I huffed out a breath. "Briar, cool it. I'll see you both tomorrow. Get some sleep. Don't worry. I'm the big sister around here, remember?"

They both made smoochy kiss noises. *Kill me now.*

"Sisters?" Monroe said. "I've got a younger brother."

I just smiled, not saying anything.

Then a giant shiver wracked me. Liam glanced my way, frowned, then pulled me closer to his side.

"Look, we're freezing. I'll call with a full statement tomorrow."

The officer nodded.

"I need to get Penn dry and get these cuffs off."

"I'd remove the cuffs for you," the officer said. "But those don't look like standard police issue."

Maverick made a sound. "I can remove them. I've got a toolbox in my car." He stomped off.

Liam wrapped an arm around me and led me inside his building. His friends followed.

It was a silent trip up to the penthouse. We all shuffled into Liam's living room.

"I'll get you guys some blankets." Monroe disappeared. Moments later she was back, draping us both with blankets.

I dropped onto the couch, exhausted, and let the warmth seep in. I lifted my sore foot and saw a graze. It didn't look too bad, but I made a mental note to give it a good clean.

Maverick stalked into the living area with a tough, black toolbox in hand.

"Okay, what happened?" Zane demanded. "The real story, not that sanitized one you just told the cops."

"We got run off the road and shoved into the trunk of a car. They handcuffed us, took us to an abandoned warehouse by the water in Brooklyn, and tied us to chairs."

"Who were *they*?" Maverick lifted some bolt cutters.

"We didn't really have time for chitchat," Liam said.

"But you suspect someone," Zane said.

Maverick cut the handcuff chain, leaving the metal bracelets on our wrists.

"Freedom," I said.

Then the tech billionaire pulled out another tool. I had no idea what it was. I heard a buzz, and saw the vibrating blade glow orange, and realized it was some sort of high-tech saw.

"A little experimental prototype of mine." Maverick soon cut through the bracelet on Liam's wrist. He turned to me and I held up my hand.

"I'm not going to 'accidentally' lose a finger, am I?" I asked.

The big man grunted.

He cut the metal off, and I rubbed my red wrist. "Thanks."

The billionaires and Monroe were watching us. I felt the need to fidget.

"You can trust them."

It was Monroe who'd spoken. I looked up, and saw the woman staring at me.

"Whatever trouble you're in, you can trust them."

God. "It's not that." I weighed the odds. Erica would leave the decision to me, but I was conscious that I held Jake's life in my hands.

I couldn't imagine these men would rush out and blow my investigation. They were just worried about their friend.

"Aspen?" Liam asked.

Maverick frowned. "Aspen?"

I juggled the blanket and pulled it tighter around me. "My name isn't Penn Channing. It's Aspen Chandler."

Maverick's dark brows drew together, and Zane frowned.

Liam took my hand and squeezed my fingers.

I realized he could've been hurt tonight. Or worse. I was damn glad we were both breathing and sitting safely on his couch.

I swallowed. "I'm not a blackmailer—"

Maverick crossed his arms.

"I'm a private investigator."

You could have heard a pin drop.

"I'm undercover, investigating a white-collar-crime gang called Nexus. They specialize in insurance fraud, kidnapping, and —"

"Blackmailing wealthy people," Zane finished.

I nodded.

"Fuck." Maverick spun, hands on his hips.

Monroe smiled. "A PI. *Badass.*"

"We need you to keep this to yourselves. My client's

husband is being held by Nexus. She works for Liam and they demanded she spy on him. She came to me for help. One wrong move, and Nexus could kill Jake. They believe I'm Penn Channing, and that I have Liam on the hook. They want him to sign over a warehouse in the Bronx."

Maverick frowned. "They didn't want money?"

I shook my head.

"We can help," Zane said.

"I don't want you dragged into this," Liam said.

Zane threw up a hand. "If you're in it, then we're already in it."

"Vander's helping out," Liam said.

"So why kidnap you?" Monroe asked. "They think Penn's almost got you ready to sign over the warehouse."

"Doyle, the leader of Nexus, is suspicious as hell," I said. "He told me he'd do whatever he had to do to help *convince* Liam to sign the deed to the warehouse over."

"How dangerous is he?" Zane asked.

"Dangerous." Another giant shiver hit me.

"We need hot showers and to clean up." Liam rose. "Then Aspen needs to get home."

"To her sisters." Monroe smiled.

Finally, Liam's friends left.

"Come on," he said. "You need a hot shower."

I almost moaned out loud at the thought.

In his bathroom, he flicked on his huge shower. "I'll find you some clothes. Take your time."

I stared at him.

Everything that had happened closed in on me. We could've been hurt tonight, or killed.

Liam Kensington was a good man. He'd helped me, protected me, and stayed by my side. Sure, he'd been handcuffed to me, but I knew deep down that he wouldn't have left me.

My throat was tight and I swallowed.

I closed the distance between us.

He stilled.

I started unbuttoning his shirt, uncovering the golden skin of his chest.

"Aspen?" His voice was low, husky.

I met his gaze. "Don't go."

With a low groan, he yanked me close and kissed me.

13

THE BEST KIND OF BLACKMAIL

Liam

L iam's brain stopped functioning.

Aspen's mouth was on his, the taste of her filling him.

And firing up other needs.

Everything that had happened to them settled in his gut, and caught fire.

Both of them were safe.

Both of them were alive.

It was time to make the most out of that. Time to finally make this intriguing, smart, confident, and maddening woman his.

Liam wanted his hands on her flesh. Wanted her cries in his ears. Wanted her hot and wet on his cock.

"Liam—"

He gripped her jaw, then nipped her lips. Her face was flushed, naked desire on her face.

"Are you sure?" he asked.

"I'm not sure if it's my best decision, but I'm sure that I want you."

With a growl, he kissed her again. She melted against him. He pulled her flush against him. Her lips were pliant and hungry, and he slid his tongue inside her mouth, then swallowed her throaty moan.

He went to work on the rest of her clothes. Soon, her trousers and shirt were gone. She was wearing a blue bra and panties with a touch of lace and he slipped the bra off.

"Damn, you're beautiful, Aspen." He cupped her full breasts.

She pushed into him with a moan. Her pretty pink nipples were hard.

"Later, once we've taken the edge off, I'm going to take my time with these."

"You a breast man, Kensington?"

"With you, I'm an everything man." He touched her cheek, then her collarbone, then cupped her ass. "I find all of you enchanting."

She stared at him—wonder and need on her face. "I don't think anyone's ever described me as enchanting."

He fingered the side of her panties, then pushed them down. He heard her shaky intake of breath.

He toyed with the neat patch of blonde hair at the juncture of her thighs. "I'm going to spend time here too, darling. This pretty pussy, I want to know how it tastes, how hard it squeezes my cock."

She moaned. "You're the elegant billionaire, you're not supposed to be a dirty talker."

He leaned down and nipped her lip.

"I'm going to have you screaming for me, Aspen. Now—" he spun her "—in the shower."

She stepped under the water. He heard her soft moan, then she started to wash her hair.

Liam shed his shirt. He had a few scrapes and bruises, but nothing too bad. He unfastened his trousers and pushed them off. He turned, and saw Aspen watching him through the glass. Her hungry gaze roamed his chest, abdomen.

"Like what you see?"

"Yes." She pressed a hand to the glass and her eyes darkened.

With each beat of his heart, desire was a hard pulse through Liam. He shoved his black boxers off. His already-rock-hard cock sprang free.

He stepped into the shower behind her.

When she moved to turn, he held her in place, his front pressed to her back. His cock nestled against her toned ass.

Water rained over them. She smelled like his soap.

He squeezed some shower gel into his hand quickly washed himself—he wanted any remnants of the river gone.

Next, he poured more gel on his palm and smoothed it down her arms, then cupped her breasts.

"Yes." She moaned, her sleek body rubbing against his.

He slid his hand down her belly, felt her quick intake of breath, her muscles tensing. "Spread your legs for me, darling."

Her breathing turned choppy, but she did as he asked.

"Are you wet for me, Aspen?"

"*Yes.*"

He skimmed his hand down between her legs. Then he pushed two fingers inside her tight pussy.

"*Oh, God.*" Her head flew back against his shoulder.

"Aspen." His own desire was hot and out of control, battering inside him.

He thrust his teasing fingers into her, his thumb finding her slick clit.

The throb of his cock was relentless. He was going to lose his mind if he didn't have her soon.

"Liam... I'm close."

"You're not coming on my fingers the first time, my darling Aspen. You come with my cock deep inside you."

He pulled his fingers free. She turned and pressed her mouth to his chest. She bit his pec.

He groaned. His cock pressed to her belly, and as her mouth moved on his skin, her soapy hands found his cock.

Bloody hell.

She pumped him with slick fingers. His cock pulsed against her fingertips.

"So hard," she murmured. "Even your cock is handsome and elegant."

"You want my cock, Aspen?"

"Yes," she breathed.

He had no condoms in the shower, so he quickly turned the water off, then lifted her off her feet.

She gasped.

He carried her to the large marble vanity, and set her on the edge.

Damn, she was gorgeous. Her hair looked darker when wet, her skin slick, and that tight, athletic body begged to be touched.

He nudged her legs apart. Then he opened the drawer beside them and found some condoms. He tore one packet open.

She watched him slide it on.

"You are perfection," she said.

"No one's perfect."

"You're close. Like Adonis. Like some perfect marble statue come to life."

"Well, one part of me feels as hard as marble."

She laughed, but when he dragged the head of his cock through her slick wetness, it turned into a strangled moan.

"Damn, look what you've done to me, Aspen." He was as hard as steel.

She shifted back, one hand gripping the edge of the marble. The other clutched at his bicep.

"Do it," she said. "Fill me up, Liam."

He groaned. "Watch." For some reason, it felt important that she watched when he joined them.

He pushed inside her. They both watched her body take his cock.

"Ah, *God*." She tensed.

He pulled back, then thrust all the way inside her. Her cries echoed off the tiles. Like a man possessed, he started thrusting into her. "Take me. All of me."

"Yes, *yes.*" She wrapped her arms around him and met his thrusts.

He gripped her hips. His mouth was on hers, then he dragged it down her throat, bit her.

"*Liam.*"

"You're mine now, darling, aren't you?"

Her inner muscles clenched on his cock. "*Yes.*"

Fuck. He wouldn't last long.

He slid a hand between them and found her swollen clit. He flicked it, then moved lower. He stroked where she was stretched around his thrusting cock.

"You fit me perfectly. Made for me." He rubbed her clit again.

"Liam!" She threw her head back, her orgasm tearing through her.

Her body spasmed, then her pussy was milking him.

Damn. *Fuck.* Liam stiffened, and his own climax hit. He groaned, thrusting deep as his cock pulsed and he came inside her.

Aspen

Oh, boy.

When I made a mistake, I went big.

Right now, with my body loose, and liquid pleasure still filling my belly, it was hard to dredge up much regret.

Liam dropped a kiss to my lips. "Don't move."

He pulled out and I felt every inch of him. I moaned a little and bit my lip.

With a smile, he strode to the trashcan, taking care of the condom. I took the opportunity to admire his firm ass.

The man was built lean and delicious. And he knew how to pleasure a woman. Very well. I shivered. I wasn't sure I could move off this vanity anyway. I was pretty sure my legs wouldn't hold me.

He came back. *Mmm*, I wasn't sure if I preferred the front view or the back of him more.

"Warm now?" he asked with a smile.

"Yes."

"Good." He scooped me up. I really, really liked him carrying me. Did women have some deep, primitive thing about liking when a man carried her around? Maybe it was left over from caveman days?

He carried me to his bed and set me down. I stretched out and he laid down beside me.

"You look smug," I said.

"I just got what I've wanted from the first moment I saw you take that man down at Zane and Monroe's charity event. You naked in my bed."

He'd wanted this from the first moment? "It's a nice bed." I stroked the covers. Then I let my gaze drift up that delicious body of his.

"Anything else you like?" He stretched out beside me.

I crawled over to him and ran my hand up the corded muscles of his thigh. Then I tickled my fingers across his abs. His cock started swelling again, and I scratched the skin on his stomach lightly with my nails.

"Maybe," I murmured.

He made a low, sexy sound.

"Well, I think in order for me to give you what you want," I said silkily, "you should give me something in return."

I took the hot, velvet length of his cock in hand and stroked.

He made a deep sound. *Yes, growl for me, Liam.*

"Are you blackmailing me again, Ms. Chandler?"

"Yes. The best kind of blackmail."

"You put that mouth of yours on me, and I'll give you anything you want."

"That's a tempting offer." I stroked him, then lowered my head.

God, *God.* I sucked the swollen head of his cock into my mouth. *Mmm.* He jerked up, his cock filling my mouth. I slid my tongue along the underside, and took him as deep as I could.

"Fuck, Aspen." His words were a growl.

I watched his hand twist in the covers, and I kept working him, sucking him hard.

God. Watching his face, seeing the pleasure I gave him, it was intoxicating. I felt a rush of damp between my legs, and a gnawing emptiness. I needed it filled.

His hand tangled in my hair and he lifted my mouth off him.

"I'm coming deep inside you. With your pussy clenching on me."

"Okay," I panted. "Now, time for what I want."

His eyes glittered. "Name your price."

I grinned. "I want to be on top."

"I'm not going to put up a fight." He held a condom packet up.

"I like a well-prepared man." I opened it and rolled the latex on him.

"Bloody hell." His body was taut, vibrating. A look of scorching desire crossed his face.

I straddled him, my hands to his hard chest. I wanted to lick him all over. I wanted to memorize every inch of that golden skin. I bent down, grazing my teeth along his collarbone.

His hands cupped my ass and I moved, rubbing myself against him. I felt his cock move through the damp curls between my legs.

He bit out a curse.

Liam Kensington wasn't elegant in bed. He was hot. A little dirty. I loved it.

I kept rubbing against him, feeling the sensation on my clit.

"*Aspen.*" His fingers bit into my ass. "Sit on my cock."

I moaned.

"Take me deep inside you, and let me see how much you like it."

I met that searing blue gaze. I felt hot, feverish, my belly coiled tight. I saw heat and hunger reflected in his eyes.

I wished he could belong to me. Be mine.

He was for now. In this moment. At least for one night.

I lifted my hips, then lowered myself on his cock. I gasped. I felt so stretched as I eased down on his hard length, sliding him inside me.

"*Liam.*"

"Darling, you feel so good clenched around me."

I moaned and sank down, taking the last few inches of him. We both groaned.

"There it is," he said, voice gritty. "We fit so well. Now ride me."

"Quit being bossy," I panted. "I'm on top."

He gave my ass cheek a light slap. "You might be on top, darling, but you're not in charge."

We'd see about that. I started moving, rising and falling.

He sat up abruptly, with an impressive flex of his muscles. We were face to face.

It was so sexy, so intimate. I was moving on his cock, feeling him filling me, while our gazes were locked.

He kissed me, and I felt the heat growing inside me, coiling tighter.

"I'm going to come soon," I panted.

He helped me move up and down faster. "Good, because I won't last much longer. *Fuck.* You're so good, so damn tight."

He moved a hand between our straining bodies, and his finger found my clit.

I cried out.

"You look so damn good riding me, Aspen. *Faster.*"

I moaned.

"Look at me," he growled.

I did. There was so much in those blue eyes, and I couldn't look away.

"Ride me. All the way."

I moved faster, driving him deep. Then my climax engulfed me.

Arching, I screamed his name.

Liam gripped my hips harder, thrusting his body up. I heard him groaning through his own powerful release, then he buried his face in my neck.

14

GANGSTER TREASURE

Liam

Liam woke to Aspen's mouth traveling down his body. Her blonde hair spilled across his chest. When he shifted and made a rumble in his chest, she looked up.

"Well, when I make a mistake, I commit to it," she said.

He slid a hand into her hair, and tugged her face up. "We are *not* a mistake."

Her eyes flashed. "Liam—"

He rolled and pinned her beneath him.

"This is not a mistake, Aspen. Not earlier, not now. And not moving forward."

Desire and need rushed through him. He was a little stunned at how much he wanted her, after having her so many times already.

Strong, self-sufficient Aspen.

He kissed her, and it was a little hard, edgy. He let her take a lot of his weight. He wanted her to feel him.

To know he had her and wasn't letting go.

"Hold on to me," he growled. "Touch me."

She bit his lip. Her hand tangled in his hair, then she slid the other one down his back.

When she tried to quicken the kiss, he forced her to stay slow.

He wanted to savor. "We're not rushing this time." He'd had her three times during the night—each time fast, furious, scalding.

This time, he wanted to show her more.

He lifted off her, and took care of the condom. He gripped her wrists and pushed them to the bed above her head. His gaze snagged on her tattoo, and he leaned down and kissed her inked skin.

She made a choked sound.

He shifted to hold them with one hand, and used his other hand to press her thigh tight against his side. With one thrust, he slid inside her.

She gave a long, throaty moan.

"Yes," he said. "Feel that, feel me, feel *us*. I want you to feel me here all day today, and remember me."

After that he moved faster and there was no more time for words. The room filled with gasps and the slap of flesh.

"*Liam*." Her body bowed under him.

He watched her come, pleasure stamped on her face.

Damn, she was the most beautiful thing he'd seen.

As her body clenched down on his, it triggered his

own orgasm. He groaned through the violent rush of pleasure.

Collapsing to the side, he pulled her close.

They stayed there for a while, bodies coming down and breathing returning to normal. He wished they could stay there all day, but he knew that wasn't an option.

"Right, our plan now is to shower, eat breakfast, and then we need to get to the office."

She mumbled something unintelligible.

"Aspen?"

"It's Saturday," she muttered. "And we were *abducted* last night, remember?"

"I know, but I have a couple of calls scheduled and Eleanor is coming in. I often work for a few hours on Saturday."

"And I thought I was a workaholic."

His cell phone rang, and smiling, he stroked a hand down her back. He reached for the phone and saw Vander's name on the display. He straightened.

"It's Vander."

She sat up, and pulled the sheet up to her chest.

Liam thumbed the phone. "Vander."

"Liam. I've got some information for you."

"Good. We had a pretty rough night."

"You okay?" Vander asked.

"Nexus snatched Aspen and me. We escaped from a warehouse in Brooklyn."

Vander cursed. "They aren't fucking around. They're dangerous, and you need help."

"I have a security team—"

"We both know you have excellent corporate security, but you need someone with a different skill set." Vander paused. "I can't get away right now, but I know a guy. He's former Ghost Ops. A bit of a loner who lives up in Vermont. He's good in a fight, and he owes me a favor."

Liam looked at Aspen. He wanted her safe. "Okay. Call him. Now, the warehouse?"

"You said Nexus punched holes in the oldest part of the warehouse," Vander said. "So, I had Ace take the searches back further."

"You got a hit," Aspen said.

"Hi, Aspen. Yes, we did. The warehouse is linked to a prohibition gangster by the name of Dutch Schultz, born Arthur Simon Flegenheimer in 1901."

Liam frowned. "That rings a bell."

"The guy started out as a bouncer, but his brutal reputation got him a promotion. He ended up a partner with the local mobster in the Bronx. They expanded their bootlegging and speakeasy empire."

"We already guessed someone used that warehouse to store bootlegged beer," Aspen said.

"Right. But I don't think this has anything to do with bootlegging," Vander continued. "Schultz was also known for his lost treasure."

Liam stiffened. "Lost treasure?"

"At the end of his life, he was being heavily pursued by the authorities. Afraid he was going to get locked up, he apparently commissioned the construction of a special airtight and waterproof lockbox. It's said Schultz put seven million dollars in cash, bonds, coins, and diamonds in it."

Aspen frowned. "Seven million in the 1930s would be worth...?"

"Over a hundred and thirty million dollars today," Vander finished.

Liam frowned. "Why not just blackmail me for a hundred and thirty million dollars?"

"That's a big lump of money," Vander said. "They might think you'd hunt them down."

"But losing a few million in property, you might shrug that off," Aspen said.

Mmm, something still felt off about this.

"Supposedly, legend says that Schultz buried the treasure somewhere in the woods of rural upstate New York," Vander said. "Treasure hunters look for it out there, but no one's ever found anything."

"You think it's in the warehouse?" Aspen said.

"I think Nexus believes that," Vander said.

Shit.

"And if Nexus had the deed to the land, anything found there would legally belong to them," Aspen said.

Liam stroked his chin. "Nexus isn't the type to take a gamble on a lost treasure."

Aspen nodded. "They know something."

"My man Rome suggested you contact some people he knows in Denver," Vander said. "Declan Ward is a former Navy SEAL, and along with his brother and sister, they run Treasure Hunter Security. It's an outfit that provide security for digs, expeditions, that kind of thing. Darcy Ward is also engaged to an FBI agent who is part of the Art Crime Team. They might be able to shed some more light on this."

"Okay," Liam said.

"I'll set up a call for later today."

"Thanks, Vander."

"And expect a visit from Boone. He's a good guy, just a bit antisocial."

After Liam ended the call, he kissed Aspen's nose. "So, we might have a gangster treasure involved?"

She shook her head. "Nothing would surprise me at this point."

"Get in the shower. I'll make you some breakfast."

"And I need to stop by my place to get fresh clothes."

While she was in the shower, Liam made French toast. She came out in one of his shirts and her pants from the night before.

Her eyes widened. "French toast?"

He'd topped it with fresh raspberries and cream.

She dug in and let out a long moan. "This is *so* good. Will you marry me?"

He sipped his coffee and watched color fill her cheeks. "Yes."

She choked, and grabbed her glass of juice and drank a long gulp.

Liam found he liked the idea of Aspen Chandler in his life long-term.

She eyed him warily. "I... Um... I wasn't really asking."

He let his smile widen. "I'd be happy if you just moved in for a while, first."

Her green eyes went wide. "You're just messing with me, right?"

He rested his elbows on the island and leaned over

and kissed her nose. "You're the crack PI, what do you think?"

"I think I'm going to eat the rest of this fabulous French toast and ignore you."

He let her off. *For now.*

But once this thing with Nexus was over and Jake Knox was home safely, Liam decided she was moving in. He'd need a strategic plan to convince her.

"I'll shower and change. We'll stop by your place, get to the office, and then talk to this FBI agent and the Treasure Hunter Security people."

***

Aspen

On the way to the office, I sent Erica an update. I really wished I had time to see her, reassure her, but the deadline Doyle had given me was ticking down in my head.

The best thing I could do for Erica was bring Jake home.

I'd seen my sisters for thirty seconds when I'd raced home to change. They'd peppered me with questions through my bedroom door—where had I been, who did I spend the night with, and was the sex good?

The sex was mind-scrambling, tingle-inducing good.

Anyway, I'd escaped Juno and Briar as fast as I could. If they ever got wind of Liam, they'd lose their minds.

The office was quiet, although despite it being Saturday, there were a few enterprising people at their desks. The steely-eyed Eleanor looked just as polished as always. When Liam told her that he needed me for a special project, I could tell the woman wasn't buying our cover story.

Well, I couldn't exactly tell her it wasn't personal. Since the man had made me come—well, I'd lost count of how many times exactly.

No, this was *really* personal.

We settled in his office and Liam had gotten onto his first call. He was talking with someone in London, and I found it sexy that his British accent deepened as he talked.

Right now, he stood in profile to me, pacing a little as he talked. *So handsome and sexy*.

For a little while, I would take what he gave me. Maybe if I made enough memories with him, they'd sustain me when he walked out of my life.

Men like Liam Kensington could have anything and anyone. Liam and I were sharing the same orbit right now, but I hardly belonged in his space, breathing his air.

This thing would flare out, then he'd realize that I wasn't polished or sophisticated, and that I wasn't that intriguing after all, and he'd walk away.

And I was starting to suspect that I'd be left with a battered heart afterward.

The man was under my skin, and burrowing deeper every minute.

"Aspen?"

I looked up. He was watching me carefully.

"We have a call in twenty minutes with the Treasure Hunter Security guys."

I nodded. I was sitting in front of his big desk. I had a

tablet out, with all the information on Dutch Schultz and his treasure.

"You really think this treasure is sitting in a rotten warehouse in the Bronx?" I asked.

Liam moved in front of me, and leaned back on the desk. I let my gaze run up his body. The man was sexy enough already, but the suit made him even more so.

"Doyle must believe it," Liam said.

"Everything I can find says it's hidden upstate, in the woods, by a river. That's what Schultz rambled about on his deathbed."

"Maybe it isn't. Maybe that's why it's never been found."

"Look." I rose and sat on the desk beside him. "This is what's in the lockbox."

Liam whistled. "I can see why Nexus wants it." He reached out and touched my cheek. "I like your outfit."

When he'd taken me to my place, I'd made him stay outside in the car. I'd quickly changed into a long, blue skirt and scoop-necked, black top with long sleeves.

"A-hem, we're working."

"And I'm the boss, so I make the rules."

"You weren't the boss when I was riding you a few hours ago."

He smiled. "Yes, I was." He leaned closer. "And I'm having all kinds of ideas inspired by you, darling, and my desk, and that skirt rucked up around your hips."

"You shouldn't get involved with your employees, Mr. Kensington," I said primly.

He snorted. "You're not my employee. We're working together."

His perfectly shaped lips were a whisper from mine. I wanted to close the distance between us. Desire was hot and churning in my belly.

I leaned closer.

Suddenly, the office door was flung open. Liam jerked back.

I scrambled off the desk, sending the tablet to sleep to hide the information on the screen.

A suit-clad Rupert Kensington strode in and smirked at us.

Eleanor hovered in the doorway, a harried look on her face. "I'm so sorry, Liam."

"It's okay, Eleanor."

The assistant shot Liam's father an acidic look, then closed the door behind her.

He eyed me up and down, an ugly smile on his face. I didn't think he recognized me from the event at Gotham Hall.

"You're fucking an employee." Rupert shook his head. "Such a hypocrite, Liam. You lord that holier-than-thou attitude over me, but you're just like the rest of us."

Liam stepped forward, but I grabbed his arm. "He's riling you."

Liam stopped and sucked in a breath. "What are you doing here, Father?"

"I wanted to see my son."

"What are you doing here?" Liam repeated.

"I have a business deal that I want—"

"Not interested."

Rupert's face twisted. "You think you're better than me. The *perfect* Liam Kensington."

I saw Liam's jaw harden.

"You aren't better than me. It's my blood running in your veins."

"I know." A muscle ticked in Liam's jaw.

What? Did he really believe that bullshit? He was *nothing* like his father.

"Hey, he is *nothing* like you," I snapped. "You are nothing like him."

Both men's heads spun to face me. They looked alike—gold hair, cut jaws, clean cheekbones—and I wondered how much that had messed with Liam's head over the years.

I pinned Rupert with a stare. "You're an asshole with the predilection for shady deals and young girls."

I saw the rage flare. He took a step forward.

Liam stepped in front of me.

Rupert's face twisted. "You're just cheap pussy. You don't know me."

I laughed. "You have no idea who I am. You're one of those men who sees what he wants to see. Him—" I pointed at Liam. "He sees everything. Stuff I don't even want him to." Our eyes met. "He sees beyond the surface, to what matters. He's a good man, doing good things. You'll never be able to say that. Your blood might be in his veins, but he is his own man."

Liam grabbed me, giving me a searing look that made my chest hitch.

Then he kissed me.

I drank him in and kissed him back.

"I really, really like you," he said.

"I like you, too," I murmured.

"This is *outrageous*," Rupert spat. "I won't let this piece of trash talk to me like this."

"I've seen the pictures, Father," Liam said.

His icy voice made me shiver.

Rupert frowned. "Pictures?"

"Of you with four underage girls. They took pictures, Father."

All the color drained from Rupert's face. "I have no idea—"

"Don't even try to deny it. They're threatening to release them."

Rupert scraped a hand over his mouth. I could see his brain working overtime.

"What do they want? Money?"

"It's more complicated than that," Liam said.

Rupert lifted his chin. "I suppose you'll enjoy watching me go down."

Liam sighed. "No. And I'm doing what I can to stop them."

Hope flared. "Liam...I—"

"I'm not doing it for you. I'm doing it for Mom, and Annabelle, and for your children. For those girls you molested. You think that this only affects you?"

I could see that Rupert hadn't thought of anyone but himself.

"It's best you leave, Father."

Rupert sniffed. "I'm leaving. You won't see me again." He sailed out of the office.

"I wish that was true," Liam murmured. "He's said that to me so many times before."

"Screw him. And if you think that you are anything like him, you're not as smart as I thought."

A faint smile touched his mouth. "You're a little over-protective. I like it."

"Do you really think you have anything in common with that man?"

"I see him in my face. My mother likes to tell me that I'm cut from the same cloth as him. I think she's waiting for me to get caught in a sex scandal."

"Bullshit," I spat.

Liam nipped my lips. "Yes, I like everything about you, Aspen Chandler."

"I can't cook."

"Luckily, I can."

"I'm messy sometimes."

"I have a housekeeper."

"I can be abrupt—"

"I like that."

"Liam..."

The phone on his desk pinged. Eleanor's voice came through the intercom. "Liam, you have a video call from Denver. A Special Agent Alastair Burke."

Liam touched my chin and straightened. "Please put him through."

15

SHADES OF GRAY

Liam

Liam sat behind his desk, and Aspen pulled up a chair beside him.

The laptop screen blinked to life.

Three people appeared on screen—two men, and an attractive brunette with dark hair cut in a bob style, and blue-gray eyes that twinkled with intelligence.

One man stood behind the woman and had the same eyes as her, so Liam guessed instantly that this man was her brother. He was dressed in jeans and an olive-green T-shirt, and gave off the same military vibe that Vander did.

The man sitting beside the woman wore a suit and had an assessing gaze. He'd be the FBI agent.

The man in the suit spoke. "I'm Special Agent Alastair Burke. This is Declan Ward." He jerked his head to the other man. "And Darcy Ward, my fiancée."

Liam had been right on all counts.

Declan Ward gave them a chin lift, and Darcy waved.

"Thanks for talking with us. I'm Liam Kensington, and this is Aspen Chandler. Sorry to intrude on your Saturday."

Burke inclined his head. "Not a problem."

"Vander briefed you?"

"Yes. I'm sorry about your troubles." Burke paused. "I'd suggest you take this to the FBI—"

Aspen leaned forward. "That's not an option. A man's life is on the line."

"We get it." Declan Ward's voice was a rumble. "We've dealt with similar situations before."

"Vander thought you might be able to help with Dutch Schultz's treasure," Liam said. "We suspect Nexus, the criminal group we're dealing with, knows something that led them to my warehouse."

"And you could help us understand why they want this treasure so badly." Aspen shrugged. "I mean, they could've just asked Liam for money. He's got a lot of it."

Burke leaned forward. "I have a file on the Schultz treasure. Treasure hunters have been looking for it for years. There are reports of it being buried in the Catskills. There are several old eyewitness accounts of men in fedoras burying something by Esopus Creek near Phoenicia."

Darcy shifted. "A couple of treasure hunters with metal detectors found two gold coins dating from the right time in the Catskills."

Liam frowned. "So you think Nexus is off-base with the warehouse?"

"No," Burke said. "Schultz was obsessed with protecting his wealth."

"And those treasure hunters were making a documentary," Darcy added dryly.

Aspen nodded thoughtfully. "Or Schultz was smart enough to try and throw people off the real location."

"When Schultz died," Burke said, "it came out that his wife wasn't actually his wife."

Liam frowned, uncertain what this had to do with the treasure.

"It turned out that Schultz already had a wife. People expected her to come forward for her share, but she never did."

"Maybe she was terrified of him," Aspen said. "Guy was a gangster. He sounds like he had a temper and wasn't afraid to hurt people."

Liam turned this over in his head. "Or he'd already set her up."

Darcy nodded. "He never divorced her. He was living with another woman, but he never divorced his wife. Makes me curious."

"Schultz's deathbed ramblings are the stuff of legends," Burke continued. "People have written books about them, plays. People have analyzed his words for clues, but they never lead anywhere."

"No one looked for his first wife." Darcy's grin was wide. "But *I* did."

"Darcy is a bit of a whiz with computers," Burke said with a faint smile.

Liam smiled. "I have a friend like that."

Darcy snorted. "I'm probably not in the same stratosphere as Maverick Rivera."

Burke ran a hand down Darcy's back. "Don't sell yourself short."

The man was pretty straight-faced, but the adoration for his woman was clear in his eyes.

"Anyway, I found Helen Clark. She grew up with Shultz in the Bronx, and was a single mother of one son."

"Really?" Aspen said.

Darcy nodded. "She left a diary when she died, and referenced an Arthur as the father of her son."

"Schultz's real name was Arthur," Liam said.

"That's right," Darcy said. "Arthur Simon Flegenheimer. Helen's son was also Arthur. It's also mentioned that Schultz had given her a diamond."

Aspen leaned closer. "It's rumored that there are diamonds in the lockbox."

Burke nodded. "Helen sold her diamond. It was flawless, and its clarity is consistent with the old diamonds from India. It had a faint blue tint, and she'd been told that it had been cut from a larger stone."

Liam felt that tingle he got when a good deal presented itself. "You know something about this diamond?"

The FBI agent was silent for a moment. "Yes. I suspect that's why Nexus is really after the lockbox. Schultz got his hands on a legendary diamond called the Great Mogul Diamond. It went missing years ago, and came from the Kollur Mine in India. Two-hundred-and-eighty carats of flawless diamond."

"It's always diamonds," Darcy muttered.

Burke shared a private smile with his fiancée, and Liam knew there was a story there, somewhere.

"My theory is that Schultz came into possession of the Great Mogul," Burke said. "And he had it cut up."

Liam sat back. "And now Nexus wants the diamonds."

Burke nodded. "They'd be priceless. Collectors would go crazy."

"Okay, but this doesn't help us find the lockbox," Liam said.

"Helen mentioned in her diary that she knew where Shultz put the lockbox," Darcy said.

Aspen gasped. "Where?"

"We don't know," Burke said. "Helen apparently deciphered Schultz's deathbed words, but didn't share the exact location. Helen's relatives, specifically her grandson, reported that her diary and some of her belongings were stolen recently."

"Nexus," Liam said.

"Dammit," Aspen muttered. "Another dead end."

Burke's lips quirked. "Not entirely. Her grandson is still alive. He'd be happy to meet you. He still lives in the Bronx."

"Oh, God," Aspen breathed.

"He knows everything that was in that diary," Burke added.

"Thank you," Liam said. "Your help has been invaluable."

"Good luck," Darcy said.

Behind her, Declan Ward gave them a curt nod.

They ended the call and Aspen grabbed her coat.

"Let's get that fancy car of yours and head to the Bronx. I'll call the grandson on the way."

Liam gripped her arm. "This might not pan out."

"For Jake's sake, let's hope it does."

Aspen

I followed Liam up to the slightly ramshackle brownstone. He knocked on the door.

This wasn't the best part of the Bronx, but I could see that it was slowly rejuvenating.

The door opened. An older man with gray hair, wide, dark eyes, and neat clothes answered.

"Ah, Mr. Kensington," Simon Clark said. "Come in, come in."

We walked in and I gasped. The place was a shrine to all things Prohibition Era. There were old bottles, framed photos, a fedora hat resting under glass.

"And you must be Aspen," Simon said.

I nodded. Then I noticed a framed picture of Dutch Shultz on the wall.

"My grandfather. By all accounts, a ruthless man."

Dutch didn't look like a scary, bootlegging gangster in his picture. He looked...normal.

"There is a well-known account of Dutch and his gang kidnapping a bootlegging competitor, Joe Rock. Dutch had him beaten, hung by a meat hook, then a bandage infected with gonorrhea rubbed on his face."

I winced.

Liam stared at the photo. "You don't worry...that you've inherited some of that?"

My heart clenched.

"Nature is only one piece of us, Mr. Kensington. Nurture plays a huge part too." Simon smiled. "And at the end of the day, we all make our own choices. We should be judged by our own actions." Simon looked at the photo of Dutch. "And no one is black and white. There's so much gray in all of us. As well as lots of other colors. Dutch tortured people, broke the law, but he also loved my grandmother, in his own way."

"Agent Burke told you that we're looking for the treasure?" Liam said.

"Yes, and so is a group of criminals. I suspect they were the ones who broke in here and stole my grandmother's diary." An unhappy look crossed the man's face.

"We'll try to get it back to you, if we can," Liam said.

"Thank you." Simon waved at the table. "Sit, I'll bring some tea."

He disappeared into a dated kitchen, then returned with tea and biscuits.

Simon sank into a chair. "I remember everything that was written in her diary."

"You know where the treasure is?" I asked.

He shook his head.

I frowned. "Nexus has been searching in a warehouse in the Bronx. There must be something to link the treasure with that warehouse."

"My grandmother interpreted Dutch's deathbed ramblings. She believed he was speaking in code. A code the two of them used as young lovers. Unsurprisingly, her parents didn't approve of their romance."

Liam leaned back.

Simon looked thoughtful. "Dutch mentioned soap duckets. People assumed he meant buckets. It was a code he and Helen used for the warehouse they would sneak to and meet. One Dutch later purchased."

"Oh, my God," I breathed.

"There's an old picture of it there." Simon pointed to a shelf.

I rose and studied the faded black and white image. It was Liam's warehouse in the Bronx.

My pulse raced and I met Liam's gaze. We had confirmation the treasure was in the warehouse. Now, we just had to find it.

"He also talks about chimney sweeps and swords," Simon said. "I'm not certain what that means. I'm sorry I can't help you more."

I guessed it was better than nothing. We finished our tea and thanked Simon. The drive back to Manhattan was quiet, both of us lost in thought.

"We need to search the warehouse," I said.

He nodded. "Unfortunately, there's a construction survey team there this afternoon taking measurements for the Borden Project."

I chewed on my lip. "The three-day deadline is up tomorrow, Liam. We need to search the warehouse *today.*"

He nodded. "We'll go in tonight. It might be better to do this under the cover of darkness."

My stomach turned over. Right, because running

around in a dark, gloomy warehouse at night was so much fun. "Well, I suggest you leave the Aston Martin at home if we're trying not to get noticed."

"We aren't taking your poor excuse for a car."

"There's nothing wrong with my car!"

"I'll provide a car that will blend in," he said.

I grunted. Liam Kensington couldn't blend in and look ordinary if he tried.

"We have a few hours to get prepared," he said. "Come to my place?"

"I need to check in on my sisters. They're worried." Although I desperately wanted to be with him.

"Of course." He reached out and squeezed my hand. "Whatever you need."

For a second, it felt like we were a regular couple. *Don't get too used to it, Aspen.*

It wasn't long before he turned into my neighborhood. "Park here. I like to take a long walk home, and make sure I'm not followed."

I got out of the car, and he joined me on the sidewalk.

"You don't have to get out," I said.

"I'm walking you to your door."

Stubborn man. We headed down the sidewalk. Suddenly, there was a loud crack, and I felt a bullet whiz past my ear.

This time, Liam reacted first. He tackled me to the ground.

I hit the concrete belly first. "Fuck," I muttered.

Liam shifted off me and we pressed up against a small SUV parked on the street. There was more gunfire, bullets pinging off metal. I pulled out my Glock.

"Where are they firing from?" I snapped.

"No clue," he said.

There was another barrage and we ducked down.

"We can't stay here." I heard people screaming, and saw others ducking for cover. I spotted the mouth of an alley. "*There.* I'll give cover fire, and you run."

Liam's gaze burned into me. "I'm *not* leaving you, Aspen."

"I'll be right behind you."

His eyes narrowed.

"I promise. Ready?"

He nodded.

I popped up and fired in the general direction of the shooter.

Liam took off like a track runner from the starting box. The man could move.

I watched him make it safely into the alley.

Okay. I got ready, fired, then ran.

I took a zig-zagged route to the alley. Bullets hit the concrete near my feet.

Fuck.

Adrenaline flooding me, I pushed for more speed. Then I was crashing against Liam in the darkness of the alley.

"Thank God," he breathed, hugging me tightly.

I heard a scrape of noise. We both spun, as a woman in black jeans and a black leather coat materialized.

She also had dyed black hair piled up in a messy bun on top of her head. I sucked in a breath. It was the woman from Nexus—the one who'd given me the note. Doyle's second in command, Jackie Godin.

She lifted her handgun and aimed it at me. Her blue eyes were empty, and I knew she'd killed before.

"Penn fucking Channing."

Oh, shit.

"What the hell are you doing?" I said.

"All Doyle can talk about is how brilliant you are, stringing this fucking billionaire along. I'm tired of it. *I'm* his right hand. I'm not having you steal it."

"I don't want the attention, just my cut of the profits." I angled myself a little in front of Liam.

The idiot shifted, trying to protect me.

The woman's gun tracked his way.

No. I was not letting him get hurt. I whipped my Glock up and aimed at the woman.

"You'll both die here in this dirty alley," she snapped.

"You kill him, and Doyle doesn't get what he wants."

I sensed the tension in Liam. He was coiled like a spring, watching the woman intently. He was getting ready to make a move.

My belly cramped. "Hey, asshole, are you listening?"

The woman's gun swiveled back to me. "I'll just kill you, then."

The sound of the gunfire was deafening. I leaped to the side, just as Liam launched at the woman.

No.

He executed an impressive kick and knocked the gun out of her hand. His next blow sent her crashing into a dumpster with a clang. She dropped heavily to her knees.

Her gun was just a foot away, lying on the dirty concrete. She recovered and pounced.

Damn. We couldn't run out of the alley because the

shooter could still be on the street.

Instead, I leaped on Jackie. We rolled through some trash, each trying to gain the upper hand. I poked at her eyes, and she grabbed my hair and yanked.

With a grunt, I shoved and pushed her away. I rose to my knees and found myself with a gun pointed at my chest.

The woman smiled, those soulless eyes staring at me, her finger tightening on the trigger.

Oh, God.

"No!" Liam growled.

"Stay still, rich guy, or you're both dead," Jackie snapped.

A shot echoed off the walls.

I jerked, but there was no searing pain. The woman yelped, dropped the gun, and clutched her hand.

A man emerged from the shadows, holding a Sig Sauer with experienced ease.

I tensed until he flicked me a glance, then he moved over to Jackie. I noted he moved with an easy, liquid stride and didn't make a sound. He was a man in full command of his body. He had dark-brown hair with the hint of a curl, and wore a flannel shirt over a black T-shirt, well-worn jeans, and a tan-leather jacket.

He yanked Jackie's hands behind her back, and pulled out some zip ties.

Liam helped me up.

"You okay?" The man's voice was deep, gravelly.

"Yes," I said. "Thanks."

Eyes of whiskey gold met mine. "Let's get out of here."

16

USUALLY QUICK ON MY FEET

Liam

"Company will be coming," the man said. "Move."

Liam nodded, keeping his hand on Aspen's arm. "What about her?" He glared at the tied-up Nexus woman.

Aspen sniffed. "Leave her." She stepped over to the woman. "I'll be giving Doyle an update. Take this as a lesson, Jackie. I'm always prepared."

The woman just glowered at them, fury twisting in her blue eyes.

"Through here." Boone led them into a building. They hustled down a dark hallway, and somewhere, Liam heard a baby crying.

They came out at a stairwell.

The man turned. "I'm Boone Hendrix. Vander sent me."

Liam had suspected as much. "You have excellent timing, Boone. I'm Liam."

They shook hands. "I know who you are."

"And I'm Aspen."

Boone nodded, dark-brown hair falling across his forehead. "Vander briefed me."

"We got some extra information on the treasure," Liam said. "We need to search my warehouse in the Bronx tonight."

The man lifted his chin. "You need back up. I'm there." He cocked his head. "You're bleeding."

Liam touched his temple, and his hand came away with blood on his fingers.

"Oh, my God." Aspen pushed in close, her face panicked. She yanked his head down. "Oh, my God."

"I must've got nicked by debris when the bullet hit the bricks."

Boone held out a clean handkerchief.

Aspen snatched it, then pressed into Liam's temple.

"I'm okay," he said.

"You're bleeding."

"Darling, I'm fine."

She let out a shaky breath, nodded. "Your shirt isn't, though."

He glanced down and spotted the blood. He sighed. "I'll run out of clothes by the time we finish with this."

A smile flirted on her lips. "Lucky you can afford to buy more." Her smile faded. "I don't like seeing blood on your skin." She dabbed at him again.

"I'm fine," he repeated.

"My place is just around the corner. I'll clean you up there." She looked up at Boone. "Can you meet us at the warehouse at 9:30 PM?"

The big man nodded. "Text me the address." He gave them his cell number.

With a wave, Boone disappeared. Liam let Aspen drag him out of the building. They walked two blocks, then she led them into a nice, pre-war, brick building.

"You've got a good building, here," Liam said. It was second nature for him to assess a property.

"My father's parents left me this place."

"Very fortunate for you."

"Absolutely, or I couldn't have afforded to live in this part of the city." She shot him a teasing look. "We can't all buy fancy penthouses."

They walked up the central, open staircase, and he heard a door open.

"Aspen, is that you?" a shaky voice asked.

"Shit," Aspen muttered, pausing on the stairs. Then she raised her voice, half shielding Liam with her body. "Yes, Mrs. Kerber. How are you today?"

"I'm fine." The old lady squinted at them. She held a white cat tucked under one arm, and Liam could have sworn it glared at them. Shit, the thing looked evil.

"How's Skittles?"

"Oh, he's in his cage today. Do you have a young man with you?"

Aspen made a strangled sound while Liam tried to think if anyone had called him a young man in recent times.

"Yes," Aspen said. "Um, it's work related."

"Good afternoon," Liam said.

Mrs. Kerber smiled. "Oh, such a lovely accent. I dated a Brit once, before I met Mr. Kerber."

Aspen shoved Liam up the stairs ahead of her. "We really have to go. I'll see you later, Mrs. Kerber."

She unlocked her door and practically pushed Liam inside.

"Luckily she's half blind without her glasses," Aspen said. "Anyone home?"

Silence greeted them and he heard Aspen release a sigh of relief.

"Who's Skittles?" he asked.

"Mrs. Kerber's bird. She lets him out and he escapes sometimes. I usually find him for her."

"Aspen Chandler, rescuer of abducted people, black-mailed billionaires, and lost birds."

She wrinkled her nose.

He walked into her place, keen to see it. He was assaulted by greenery. There were clean, white walls, lots of comfy, unfussy lines. There was a big couch that said, "come sit a while", and plants everywhere—big ones, small ones, draping ones. Some were in giant pots, others in small, decorative urns.

He felt a sense of peace. There were pops of color here and there. A pink jacket tossed over a chair. A spill of books and magazines on the coffee table. A tube of lipstick on the kitchen counter. The kitchen had a tiny island, with two stools.

"Sit," she ordered.

He shed his jacket. Damn, his white shirt was a write off. Blood had dripped down and soaked into the collar. "I like your place. You have a green thumb."

"Yes. It started when I was a teenager."

"Oh?" He detected something in her voice.

She shrugged a shoulder. "I had this plant when I was young. An orchid. After my father left, I neglected it, and it withered. Then, I was determined to keep it alive. I babied it, watered it, sang to it. And then it flowered, and it was beautiful."

A young girl whose life was out of control, finding control once more through a plant.

"I was hooked after that." She pulled out a first aid kit and set it on the island. She spotted a folded piece of paper on the island, and snatched it up.

"What?" he asked.

"Oh, the twins are out with my mom. She came down to take them to an art show. They won't be home until late. Phew."

He felt a spurt of annoyance. "So you can sneak me out of here like a dirty, little secret."

She frowned at him. "It's not that. You're a freaking billionaire, Liam. Your presence would generate a whole bunch of questions I don't want to answer right now."

Patience, Kensington. He took a deep breath.

Aspen tore open a wipe, tipped antiseptic on it. "Hold still." She cupped his cheek and dabbed at the cut on his temple.

He saw the words inked on her forearm. Words that said so much about her. He looked at that sexy dimple in her chin, then cupped her cheek. They could have both been shot today. Flying bullets tended to put things into very sharp focus.

Made a person realize what was important.

Her gaze moved to his. Damn, she was so beautiful.

"So, your mom and sisters are out late?" he said.

"Yes."

"And we don't need to meet Boone at the warehouse for hours."

She leaned closer, gripping the collar of his shirt. "Yes."

"You haven't shown me your bedroom, yet."

She pressed her tongue to her teeth. "No, I haven't."

He tugged her against him.

"Liam, we were just shot at—"

"I know. It makes me want to celebrate being alive." He nipped her lips. "And celebrate having the sexiest, most competent woman I know under my hands."

He took her mouth. Damn, every time he kissed her was like a punch to the gut.

He pulled her closer to straddle him, then rose. She clamped her arms and legs around him.

"Which room is yours?" he asked.

She waved a hand.

He strode through the neat living space. As he walked into her bedroom, he turned his head. She nipped at his jaw.

"I like your bedroom." He did. There were lush plants, and a serene feel. Candles and more plants rested on a shelf.

"Thanks. It's my little haven."

Liam put one knee on the bed and lowered her to the pretty, soft cover.

"Now, let's christen this bed of yours." With a smile, he pressed his mouth to hers and started to unbutton her shirt.

Aspen

I collapsed on top of Liam, panting, pleasure still flooding me.

He ran a lazy hand up my back and I shivered.

"Well, I'm glad you like my room," I murmured.

His fingers danced over the knobs of my spine. "I really like you."

God, I was totally going to fall for this guy. *Danger, danger.*

"Hungry?" I asked.

"Yeah."

"I'll order takeout. There's a great Chinese place around the corner." Man, I hoped billionaires liked Chinese food.

"Sounds great."

I pressed a kiss to his chest and pushed up.

I grabbed my robe and wrapped it around my body. When I looked back, he was watching me. His gaze said he liked what he saw.

He was sprawled there in my bed, looking all golden, like a well-satisfied lion.

I escaped, telling myself that I should be guarding my heart more carefully. I rummaged through the drawers in the kitchen and found the takeout menu. Snatching up my cell phone, I placed the order.

Mmm, I needed some fried rice. The thought immediately reminded me of Erica. My friend loved fried rice, and we'd often gorged on it when we'd had sleepovers. Then I thought of Jake.

A shot of guilt closed my throat. I'd just had amazing sex, and was spending time with Liam, planning to eat Chinese. I pressed a hand to the counter and dragged in a breath. Meanwhile, Erica and Jake were suffering, and having a horrible time.

Tonight, I was going to find that lockbox. I would work it all out, dammit. I'd lure Doyle out and get Jake back, get those photos for Liam, and then watch Nexus go down.

"Hey." Liam appeared. "You look way too serious for a woman who just had two orgasms."

He was shirtless, just in his suit pants. My mouth watered. This was my favorite look of his.

He rounded the tiny island and pulled me into his arms. "You keep looking at me like that, it'll be three times."

I rested my forehead against his chest and slid my arms around him. "I'm just worried about Jake. And feeling guilty that I'm enjoying you while he's a prisoner, and Erica is pregnant, alone, and hanging on by a thread."

Liam hugged me tighter. "We're going to get him back. I'm here to help."

I looked up. "I'm not used to having help."

He gave me a dry look. "I would never have guessed. You're frighteningly competent, and wade in to help everybody."

This time, I kissed him. The man tasted better than that super expensive wine of his.

Things were getting heated. He groaned, I thrust my hands into his golden hair.

Suddenly, I heard a key in the front door lock, and the murmur of voices.

Oh. *Crap.*

The door started to open.

"Get down," I hissed.

His eyebrows shot up. "What?"

"Down." I gripped his hips and urged him downward.

He dropped into a crouch behind the island.

Juno, Briar, and my mother spilled inside. My lungs froze. *Oh, God.*

"Hi." I tried to sound casual, but my voice came out sounding like a strangled cat.

They all looked my way, shedding their coats.

"I thought you guys were out until late." I looked at Mom. "Hi, Mom."

"Hi, baby."

"The art show was a dud," Juno declared.

"Totally," Bri agreed. "A monkey could do better. It was shitwaffle."

"It was not what I'd hoped for." Mom blew me a kiss, then carefully hung her coat on the hook by the door.

The twins eyed my robe and frowned.

"Why are you home?" Briar asked.

"And why are you in your robe?" Juno followed up.

"Oh, well..." At that moment, Liam stroked a hand up the back of my leg. Sensation skidded through me and I kicked him lightly. "My case is crazy. I was tired and I had some time, so I caught a quick nap. I need to head out again tonight."

And find a way to sneak my billionaire lover out of the apartment.

The twins both stared at me suspiciously.

"You look...different," Juno said.

"Yes, relaxed or something." Briar tapped her lips. "And you never look relaxed."

I made a scoffing sound.

"She has sex hair," my mom stated.

Oh, crap. I heard Liam's quiet snort and kicked him again. His hands skimmed higher up my leg, sliding under my robe.

Damn, that felt good. *No, Aspen. Focus.*

"Aspen, spill." Juno demanded. "What's going on?"

The three of them moved closer.

"Stop." I held up a hand. "I... I..." *Come on, I was a PI. I was usually quick on my feet.*

Liam rose. "I found my contact lens."

My gut coiled into a teeny, tiny ball.

My mom and sisters froze like statues. They didn't move, except that their eyes widened.

"Um..." I pushed my hair back. "This is..."

"Liam Kensington," Briar breathed.

There went my slim hope that they wouldn't recognize him.

"It's a pleasure to meet Aspen's family." He shot them his million-dollar smile.

Briar made a sound. My mother gave a little sigh. Juno just stared, mouth hanging open.

"Liam and I are working together," I said.

"Uh-huh," Juno drawled.

"Holy shitballs," Briar murmured.

Liam winked at them and I slapped his chest.

"Cool it, darling, they aren't stupid."

"He called her darling," Briar breathed.

"Oh, my God," Juno shrieked. "My sister is banging Liam Kensington."

"Juno!" I cried.

The door buzzer rang.

"That's our Chinese takeout. Briar, can you grab it, please?" I pushed Liam ahead of me. "We've got to get going."

"Oh, you should stay," my mom said, a little breathlessly.

"Can't. Work." I shoved Liam into my bedroom.

The damn man was still smiling.

I shut the door. "This is a *disaster*."

"I beg to differ."

No, he wouldn't have to endure the teasing and ribbing, followed by the sympathetic looks once he was gone.

"Put some clothes on—"

He grabbed me and kissed me. "Everything is going to be okay, Aspen."

I really wanted to believe him.

But I knew better than anyone that things didn't always work out.

17

FROM DIFFERENT PLANETS

Liam

"*This* is your idea of blending in?"

Liam looked at Aspen across the hood of the big, black, decked-out Dodge Ram.

"It's a solid American truck. We'll be totally incognito."

She rolled her eyes and climbed in.

Liam did the same. They were both dressed in black. He wore cargo pants, black Henley, and a leather jacket. Her black jeans hugged her ass, and the sight made his cock twitch.

He remembered very well how it felt to be inside her. He knew he was gone over his tough, smart, private investigator.

He drove them toward the Bronx. The truck handled horribly, and he missed the Aston. "I'm glad I got to meet your family."

She made a noncommittal sound.

He felt a sting of annoyance. "I won't be your dirty, little secret, Aspen."

"What?" She swiveled in her seat. "You're Liam Kensington. You're nobody's dirty, little anything. You're smart, gorgeous, slightly stuck-up, but a good guy. Any woman would shout it from the rooftops, if you were hers."

His hands flexed on the wheel. He noticed that she didn't mention rich.

"Except you," he said.

"You aren't mine." She looked away. "You'll be gone, and my family will pepper me with questions—"

"I'm not going anywhere," he said darkly.

She made a scoffing sound. "Liam, you're a *billionaire*, and I'm a private investigator. We aren't just from different stratospheres, we're from different planets."

Not this again. "Fuck that. I'm just a man who likes you. You're a woman I like, admire, and who I'm totally falling for."

"What?" She blinked, and held up her hand. "No."

"You can't tell me what I feel. And what I feel is more than just lust for your delectable, athletic body."

She swiveled back to face the front. "Be quiet."

"No, no I don't think I will. Be warned, Ms. Chandler, I'm going to lavish you with my attention until it gets through your thick skull."

Her head turned and she shot him with a piercing look. "I'm going to punch you."

"I like it when you're a little rough."

She huffed out a breath. "You're impossible."

They were quiet after that, and it wasn't long before they turned onto the street where the warehouse was located. Liam parked on a side street, and they quietly slipped out of the truck.

They walked down the shadowed street. One of the shadows detached itself from the others.

Liam froze and grabbed Aspen's arm.

Boone materialized. "Hey."

"You ready?" Aspen asked.

The former soldier hefted a heavy-duty flashlight and nodded at his black backpack. "Ready."

"Here." Liam held out some small earpieces. "So we can all keep in touch."

They all put the earpieces in, then the three of them slipped into the warehouse. It was silent, and all Liam could hear was the drip of water somewhere in the building.

"Let's start with where Nexus poked holes in the wall," she said.

"I'll scout around." Boone was gone like a ghost.

"He's spooky," she murmured.

He was. "Agreed."

They checked the old brick walls where Nexus had been digging, but didn't see anything.

"Let's try upstairs," Liam said.

They both headed up the rickety stairs. They were halfway up, when suddenly, Aspen gasped. There was a crack, and her foot went straight through the rotted wood.

"You okay?" Liam gripped her shoulders.

"Yeah." She yanked her foot free. They carefully navigated to the top. He waved the flashlight around, and illuminated an old filing cabinet, its drawers pulled out. There were some old, sagging tables, as well.

"I was thinking about Helen's diary and Dutch's deathbed ramblings," Aspen said.

"Yes?" Liam aimed the flashlight at the rest of the floor. Rows of support pillars disappeared into the black.

"Chimney sweeps. Dutch said something about chimney sweeps."

Liam considered, nodded. "Chimneys." He looked up.

"Yes. The roof."

He gripped her lapels, and pressed a quick kiss to her lips. "Let's get to the roof."

She touched her earpiece. "Boone, we think it might be on the roof. Meet us up there."

"Acknowledged."

Liam and Aspen headed up the stairs. When he pushed open the door at the top, a stiff wind ruffled his hair.

"Be careful where you step," he warned. "The roof looks rotten in places, as well."

"Let's check all the chimneys," she said.

Boone appeared out of the darkness. "This roof is shit. Be careful."

They spread out, checking each of the chimneys. Liam saw Aspen blow out a breath and rest her hands on her hips.

Liam didn't spot anything out of the ordinary. He glanced over at Boone. "Anything?"

The man shook his head.

"Dammit." Aspen kicked a brick. "Jake's life is on the line. It *has* to be here."

"Hey." Liam hugged her. "We aren't done yet."

"I can't let his kid grow up without a father. My friend without her husband."

"Aspen, we *aren't* giving up."

She nodded and swiped her arm across her face. "Okay. Okay. There, I've had my breakdown. Let's keep looking."

They continued their search.

"The diary mentioned a sword." She glanced around. "What could that mean?"

Boone frowned. "No idea."

"*Wait*." Liam said. "There was a picture of the warehouse at Simon's."

She nodded.

"It had a billboard on top." Liam crossed the roof and came across old brackets attached to bricks. The billboard itself was long gone, but its base remained.

Excitement crossed Aspen's face. "*Yes*. In the picture, there was definitely a billboard, and I think it had a picture of a sword on it."

Liam pulled out his phone. "I'll call him."

"It's late—"

"I'm pretty sure he'll take my call."

"Hello?" Simon's voice was sleepy, cautious.

"Simon, it's Liam Kensington. I'm sorry to be calling so late."

"Mr. Kensington, how are you?"

"I'm not bad. I have a question for you. You had a

picture of your grandfather's warehouse in the Bronx. There was a billboard on top advertising something."

"Yes. Cammilus Knives. They were one of the oldest knife manufacturers, and popular at the time. They used crossed swords as their logo."

Knives. Sword.

"Thank you, Simon."

"Does that help?"

"I hope so," Liam said.

"All I ask is that you show me the treasure when you find it."

"Count on it."

Liam slipped his phone away. "The billboard advertised Cammilus Knives. They used swords as a logo."

"Bingo." Aspen grinned. "It's here, somewhere." They circled around the old brackets where the billboard would've been.

Liam pondered. *Where would I hide a lockbox of treasure?*

Somewhere sturdy. Somewhere safe.

He studied the bricks under the billboard brackets. They were all made of the same red brick.

Wait.

On one pillar, some of the bricks were a paler color. Discolored. Or perhaps not as old.

He crouched.

"Liam?" She crouched beside him.

"Look at these bricks."

"They're different," she breathed.

"Move back," Boone said.

The man lifted a boot, then he kicked at the bricks. He kicked again.

The bricks crumbled inward.

Liam flicked on his flashlight. A second later, he saw the gleam of metal inside. "Hold this."

Aspen held the flashlight for him, and Liam reached in...and pulled out a lockbox.

"Holy cow," she breathed.

Boone shook his head. "Here." He pulled a pair of bolt cutters from his backpack, and cut the old padlock off.

Liam opened the lid.

The box was full of wads of cash, gleaming coins, and glittering diamonds.

Aspen

Wow.

I stared at the diamonds as they glinted in the beam of the flashlight.

They were brilliant, lit by an inner fire.

I met Liam's gaze.

"Call Doyle," he said. "Have him meet us here with Jake and the photos."

I nodded.

"You gonna wear a wire?" Boone asked.

I nodded again. "Doyle isn't getting anything out of this, except for a jail cell."

I thumbed the screen of my phone.

Doyle's voice came over the line. "Time's almost up, Chandler." The man's voice was as hard as stone. "Knox is a dead man, and those photos of that sick fuck Kensington Senior will go out online first thing in the morning."

"I have the lockbox."

Silence.

"I found Schultz's treasure," I continued.

All I heard was heavy breathing. "You're lying."

"I'll text you a picture. Meet me at the warehouse, and bring the photos and Jake. And none of your goons."

A long pause. "Have you been playing me, Penn?"

"Yes. My name isn't Penn. I was hired by Erica Knox to get her husband back. So, let's all get what we want, Doyle. You give me Jake, you give Kensington the photos, and you get what you really wanted all along. The lockbox."

"I don't take kindly to being lied to." His voice was icy cold.

"That's rich, considering you're a criminal. Just get here. No goons. You play me, Doyle, and your precious diamonds will end up in the bottom of the river."

"I'll be there." Doyle hung up.

I blew out a breath. "He's coming."

We all headed downstairs. I was alive with nerves. If anything went wrong...

We reached the bottom level.

Boone scanned around. "I'll make myself scarce. Signal if you need me."

"Thanks, Boone," Liam said.

He shot us a small salute, and melted into the darkness.

I turned to Liam. He took a small case from his pocket and opened it.

"Mav gave me these." They looked like simple, silver stud earrings. "They're high-tech recorders. They also transmit. They'll record everything Doyle says and upload it to the cloud."

I slipped the studs into my earlobes.

"Liam, I don't suppose I can convince you to wait in the car?" Or better yet go home. Get somewhere safe.

He shot me a sharp look. "Fuck, no."

"Fancy British billionaires are not supposed to get their hands dirty." Or put themselves in danger. My stomach skittered.

"Your billionaire rulebook is different than mine." He smoothed my hair back. "It's going to be fine, Aspen. It'll be over soon."

I didn't feel fine. I couldn't bear it if he got hurt. My stomach turned over and left me jittery. I knew Boone was somewhere, hiding in the darkness, but it didn't calm me.

We waited, and finally, I heard the screech of a metal door opening.

Liam held the flashlight pointed downward, and I held the lockbox.

The dark shadow of a man strode in, gripping a leaner, stumbling man beside him.

Doyle stepped closer to the pool of light from a flashlight, yanking his captive with him.

Jake's face was battered and bruised. The assholes

had beaten him. His hands were tied in front of him.

"Jake?" I said, trying to keep my voice level.

He lifted his head and blinked. "Aspen? God, Aspen."

"It's going to be all right." I looked at Doyle.

The leader of Nexus stepped closer, and I got a clear look at him.

Fit body, heavy features, brown hair and wide-set eyes. He was essentially nondescript. Nothing made him stand out. You'd pass him on the street and not give him a second thought.

"Doyle," I said.

"Aspen Chandler," he replied.

Ah, someone had gotten busy in the time since I called him.

Doyle jerked his head toward the box. "Show me."

I flicked open the lid, and Liam aimed the light.

Doyle's face changed—filling with eagerness, and a hungry light that made me feel edgier. It was a look that bordered on obsession.

"The diamonds," he breathed.

"From the Great Mogul Diamond," Liam said.

Doyle's head jerked up. "You know?"

Liam nodded. "Yes."

"Finally, after so many years," Doyle said.

I cocked my head. "What do you mean?"

"My real name isn't Kristoff Doyle. I was born Kristoff Flegenheimer."

I gasped. "The same surname as Dutch Schultz."

"His father and my great-grandfather were brothers— Israel and Moses. They were diamond dealers in

Germany. They made a huge find with the Mogul. Then Israel stole it, killed my great-grandfather, and escaped to the USA." Anger flashed on Doyle's face. "And my side of the family was plunged into poverty, while Israel's son turned to crime, and lived a lavish lifestyle. He also cut up the Mogul." Doyle spat the words and looked at the diamonds. "Now, I'm reclaiming what's mine."

"You're a thief too," I said angrily. "You've destroyed lives. You're no better than Dutch."

"Shut up!" Doyle shoved Jake forward and the man fell to his knees.

"Aspen. Liam." Boone's quiet murmur in our ears. "He's got people with him. They're around the perimeter. They're moving, but I can't see what they're up to."

Shit. I bit my tongue.

"Where are the photos?" Liam demanded.

Doyle tossed a large, yellow envelope on the ground. "There's a USB drive inside, as well."

Liam stared, his jaw hard. "Are all of them in there?"

"Yes." Doyle's smile was sharp. "You'll have to trust me on that, Mr. Kensington." He looked back at me. "Now give me the box, Ms. Chandler."

I held it out. I didn't want to, but I'd have to trust that Boone would nab Doyle on the way out.

Doyle flipped the lid closed. "I'd say it's been a pleasure doing business with you, but it hasn't." He touched his own ear. "*Now.*"

My pulse went crazy. *What the hell was he doing?* "Doyle—"

Boom.

Boom.

Boom.

The building vibrated, and dust rained down on us. Then the walls exploded.

Oh, fuck. I ducked. Liam threw himself over me.

We crouched on the floor. I looked up and saw Doyle disappear into the darkness.

"They've detonated explosives!" Boone sounded like he was running. "Get out!"

"Doyle's on the move." I *had* to stop him.

Liam rose and snatched up the envelope with the photos.

"Help Jake," I cried.

With a nod, Liam grabbed the man's arm. I smelled smoke, and watched as flames licked up the walls.

We all jogged together, the smoke thickening. I coughed.

"Go. *Go.*" I pushed Jake and Liam ahead of me.

There was a loud crack from above, followed by the groan of wood.

I looked up. *No.*

I shoved Liam hard. He stumbled forward, Jake falling with him.

Beams crashed down around us, flames crackling along them.

The burning debris had fallen between us. Cutting me off.

I stared across the flames at Liam.

"Aspen!" he roared.

"Get Jake out. I'll find another way."

Liam cursed. "Get your ass out, Aspen. Or I'll come back to find you."

18

I'M A CATCH

Liam

Liam kept his arm clamped around Jake, hauling the man forward. More beams crashed to the concrete floor, and the smoke thickened.

Jake coughed, hacking loudly.

"Hang in there," Liam said.

God, all he could think about was Aspen. She was trapped back there.

He had to get to her, but first he had to get Jake out.

There was more smoke—thick, oily, and black. Liam coughed. The ceiling crashed down to their left. *Shit.*

He spun Jake away. Then felt stinging on his arms and chest, and saw the fabric of his clothes burning. He slapped at it.

I...can't..." Jake wheezed.

"Come on, Jake. Think of Erica."

The man stiffened, then nodded.

They stumbled onward, and finally Liam saw a door ahead.

He flung it open. Someone rushed at them, and Liam tensed. But he quickly recognized Boone's rugged form.

"Help me with him," Liam barked.

The man got on the other side of Jake and together they hauled him out.

Fresh night air smacked Liam in the face.

So good. Boone helped Jake sit on the curb as Liam bent over and coughed. He breathed in more air.

"I'm going back for Aspen. Did you stop Doyle?"

Boone scowled. "I didn't see him come out." Boone looked up at the warehouse. "I neutralized the guys outside. They set the charges."

Fuck, maybe Doyle got trapped inside. Liam stabbed a finger at Jake. "Stay with him."

"Kensington, it's a death sentence to go back in there."

Somewhere on the upper levels, windows shattered. Liam scanned the burning building then met Boone's dark gaze.

"I'm not fucking losing her."

"Here." Boone shoved some fabric at Liam.

It was a black neckerchief.

Liam quickly tied it over his mouth.

"Don't get killed, Kensington," Boone growled.

With a nod, Liam raced back into the warehouse.

It was like hell on Earth. Flames and smoke filled the space. He crouched down and ran deeper into the building, back toward where he'd last seen her.

Come on, Aspen.

He couldn't lose her. He was obsessed. In lust. Falling in love. All of it.

In the blink of an eye, she'd become so damn important to him. She'd woken him up.

No, he wouldn't lose her.

The heat intensified, but Liam pushed on.

He had to find his woman.

Aspen

Coughs wracked me. My chest hurt so badly.

I dropped to my hands and knees and found the air slightly clearer by the floor. I dragged in a breath and started crawling.

How the hell would I get out of here?

I coughed again. I really needed to find an exit.

I saw movement and turned. *There.*

Oh, God, it was Doyle. He was backlit by the flames behind him.

I pushed myself to my feet. "You have nowhere to go, Doyle."

He spun, the lockbox clutched under his arm. His clothes were covered in soot.

"Aspen!" Liam's voice came through my earpiece. "Where are you?"

I didn't respond, I just prayed he was outside. *Safe.*

Doyle smiled at me. "It's poetic if we die here together, Aspen Chandler."

I frowned.

"When I looked you up, I recognized your father's name. He was one of my first jobs. It was so ridiculously easy to lure him into stealing from his clients."

My stomach dropped. "*No.*"

"Yes. Jeffrey and I worked very closely together. I saw you and your sisters once. You came to visit him at his office."

I wanted to vomit. *Doyle.* This man had exploded our lives apart. Shattered my family. Changed my childhood forever.

"If not for me, I'm guessing you wouldn't be a do-gooder PI." His teeth gleamed. "You've spent your entire life trying to make amends for your father's sins."

Anger exploded. With a roar, I charged and hit him. We both went down and rolled across the dirty floor. The flames were so close that I felt the heat on my skin.

Doyle rammed a fist into the side of my head, and I saw stars. I rolled again.

"Aspen!" Liam's agonized roar. "I'm *not* letting you die in here. I'm not leaving until I find you."

My pulse went crazy. *No.* I couldn't let him stay in here and get hurt.

Coming up on my knees, a moment of clarity hit me. I stared at Doyle. His face was bleeding, but he was grinning madly at me.

But he was the past.

My father had screwed up, but that wasn't on me.

Shit. I'd been telling Liam that he wasn't his father, but Doyle was right, I'd been trying to make amends for my father's crimes all my life.

"Screw you, Doyle."

I turned. I was getting out of here and finding Liam.

I wanted to live.

There was a huge crash and Doyle screamed.

I spun and saw burning wood hit him.

My gut clenched. He screamed, slapping at his burning hair.

A voice in my head told me to go. Then I shook my head and cursed.

I might be done making amends for my father, but I still had to look at myself in the mirror.

I snatched up the lockbox. *Ow.* It was hot. I tucked it against my hip. I slid my other arm around Doyle and heaved him up.

"Come on." I kept my arm locked around him. His face was raw and burned.

I had no idea which way to go. My gut lurched. I couldn't tell which direction was what. Everything around me was burning.

"*Aspen.*" Liam in my ear again.

"Liam! I'm trying to find a way out."

"Can you tell me where you are?"

Panic closed my throat. "No." The flames were all around, the air thick with smoke. Somewhere in the distance, I thought I heard sirens. "Tell me you're safe."

"I'm coming for you."

"Liam, get out, please." My chest hitched. "Liam—"

"Don't say it. I'm going to find you."

"Being with you... It's the best thing that ever happened to me."

"Bloody hell, Aspen. I'm not done with you yet. I'm falling in love with you."

My pulse spiked. "You're not supposed to do that!" My heart did a wild dance in my chest.

A support pillar collapsed. I screamed and Doyle groaned.

"Aspen!" Liam yelled.

"Everything's collapsing." I pulled in a shaky breath. "Liam, I'm falling for you too. Against my better judgment."

A strangled sound came across the line. "I'm a catch."

Despite everything, I laughed. "And so modest."

Another pillar fell.

Something smacked my shoulder and I stumbled. Doyle's weight knocked me down.

I hit the floor and started coughing, my vision wavering.

I realized I wasn't going to make it out.

"*Liam*." A hoarse whisper.

Liam

Liam leaped over some burning debris.

"Aspen! *Aspen!*"

He looked around, but all he saw were flames and smoke. His lungs were burning.

"Sorry...Liam." Aspen's voice was quiet and raspy through his earpiece. "Be...happy."

His chest caved in. "Aspen!"

He leaped another burning beam, feeling the heat

under him. He landed in a crouch. Ahead, he spotted two bodies sprawled on the ground.

Aspen.

He raced over and spun her. She looked up at him, blinking, her face dazed.

Quickly, Liam glanced over and saw Doyle, his face horribly burned. The man moaned quietly.

The lockbox was clutched in Aspen's hands.

Liam cupped her cheek. "Hey."

She blinked slowly. "Are you a golden angel?"

"It's okay, darling. I'm getting you out of here."

She blinked again. "Liam?"

He touched his earpiece. "Boone, can you get to me?"

"Where are you?" came the deep-voiced response.

"Dead center of the warehouse. There's a big pile of debris on the way in, but if you go left, you should be able to get through."

Liam grabbed the lockbox and then hauled Aspen into his arms. She blinked at him once more and then lost consciousness, her body a dead weight.

Dammit. Be okay, Aspen.

He glanced back at Doyle, wanting to leave him.

Then Liam cursed under his breath. A second later, he heard the crunch of something and spun. Boone leaped over some burning flames and landed nearby.

Liam jerked his head. "Get him."

With a nod, Boone yanked Doyle to his feet, then tossed the man over his broad shoulders.

Then they started back toward the entrance.

They made their way slowly through the warehouse, battling through the smoke and flames. To Liam, it felt like their pace was glacial. He could hear sirens outside now, and knew help was close by.

He had to get Aspen out.

He wasn't letting her die here.

He couldn't live without her.

"This way," Boone roared.

Liam swiveled, and followed the other man.

A second later, they burst outside.

Thank fuck. Emergency lights strobed through the smoke and darkness, and engines were rumbling. Firefighters in all their gear were springing into action.

Liam stumbled out onto the sidewalk, falling to his knees, cradling Aspen in his arms.

She was unconscious, her face covered in soot.

"Aspen." He pressed his face to her hair. "Help! She needs help."

19

MY HERO

Aspen

Someone was touching me.

And it hurt.

I came up swinging.

"Easy, there," a raspy female voice said. Someone caught my hand.

I blinked awake. I registered white light, a bed beneath me, and the smell of antiseptic.

Hospital.

I sagged back on the pillows, and the pleasantly-lined face of a middle-aged nurse came into view.

"You've had a hell of a night." The woman dabbed something on my neck, and I winced from the sting.

"You have a few burns, but nothing too bad. You're lucky, honey."

Burns.

Fire.

Warehouse.

I tried to sit up. "The man who came in with me, is he okay?" God, where was Liam? Had he been hurt? I scanned the room, but I was alone with the nurse. Why wasn't he here?

Suddenly, a coughing fit overtook me, my chest burning.

"Take it easy." The nurse pressed a mask to my mouth.

I breathed deeply, trying to calm my breathing.

"A few men came in with you," the nurse said. "One was in handcuffs."

I swallowed. "Not him. The blond, gorgeous one."

She smiled. "Ah, he was hard to miss. He was whisked away for treatment. Smoke inhalation. All of you were suffering from the smoke. The one in handcuffs had it the worst. He's got a bunch of third-degree burns to his face and is in surgery. The big, tough-looking guy was fine, and the other guy who'd been beaten is getting seen to."

"Okay." I pulled in a breath. "That's good news." I tried to dredge up some sympathy for Doyle, but failed.

"Since you've got a few minor burns and smoke inhalation, you're going to stay with us overnight for observation." She patted my shoulder. "Lucky you."

"No. I... The blond man. I need to see him." I needed to see with my own eyes that Liam was okay.

"I bet. Any woman would like to see more of that man." She winked.

I slid my legs over the side of the bed.

"Honey, he's in a private room, and *no one* is getting to him." She arched a brow. "Are you family?"

I hunched my shoulders. "No."

"Then, I suggest you get some rest. He'll find you if he wants to."

She turned to leave.

"Wait," I said. "He's really okay?"

I saw sympathy on her face. "I can't talk about other patients."

"I'm not asking for all the medical details."

She nodded. "He's okay."

I let out a shuddering breath, and the nurse slipped through the curtains surrounding the bed.

Liam was okay. Grasping onto that thought, I stood, and everything wavered. My hand shot out and I gripped the bed.

Crap. I had one of those stupid hospital gowns on, with my ass hanging out. There was no sign of my clothes, and I had no shoes.

It didn't matter. I was finding Liam, no matter what.

I poked my head out of the curtain and saw a male nurse walking past.

"Excuse me?"

The man looked at me. "Are you all right?"

"Um, I can't seem to find my clothes. Is there anything I can wear?"

He eyed me. "I'll see what I can do."

Back in my makeshift cubicle, I leaned against the bed and had another coughing fit. I didn't see the lockbox anywhere, so I assumed Liam had it.

God, Jake. Was he all right? I hoped someone had called Erica.

The male nurse appeared, and handed me some folded blue scrubs.

"Thanks," I said.

I quickly pulled them on, hating that my bra was gone.

Oh, well. Barefoot and braless, I headed out. Ahead, I saw the nurses' desk. A pretty nurse, maybe mid-thirties, with dark hair and dark eyes, looked at me.

"I'm looking for the people that came in with me?" I asked.

"Name?"

Shit. "Liam Kensington."

Her gaze changed and she eyed me like I was a slimy bug. "We have no one by that name."

"I know he's here. We came in together."

"Are you family?"

"No, but we—"

"I can't divulge that information."

"He'd want to see me."

"He left instructions to let no one through."

Those words were like a sharp punch to my gut.

Another woman sauntered up to the desk. She wore a sharp suit, styled hair. She screamed reporter.

"Liam Kensington's room, please?"

The nurse cocked her head. "Are you family?"

"Oh, well, almost." The woman smiled.

The nurse's face looked like stone. "We have no one by that name."

The woman in the suit stopped smiling. "There's a warehouse in the Bronx still burning, and I know one of the billionaire bachelors was brought in. The public has a right to know."

"Leave," the nurse said. "Or I'll call security."

Shit. They'd bar anyone trying to get to him.

Feeling dizzy, I wandered away. I sagged against the wall and looked at the burns on my arms, and wondered why they didn't hurt more.

Probably some good painkillers they'd pumped into me.

Nurses and doctors rushed past, pushing someone on a gurney.

I was just in the way here. I ached, I was tired, and I just wanted Liam.

I thought about hustling my way through. I could swipe a nurse's name tag and bluff my way past the desk.

But a thought hit me—if Liam was here, and he was okay, why hadn't he found me?

My stomach turned over in an uncomfortable way, and tears pricked my eyes.

He had the photos and the lockbox. I guess he didn't need anything else.

My foggy head made it hard to think. There was no way to get to him. I walked down the corridor, through some double doors, and came out in the main waiting area.

A baby was wailing, people sat slumped in chairs, and someone was moaning.

I hunched my shoulders, my chest tight. I headed for the front doors, but I had no clue what I'd do. I needed to find a phone. I could call a cab. Another wave of dizziness hit me, but this time with the added swirl of nausea. *Great.*

I weaved through some chairs, and then reached the automatic doors as they opened.

"Going somewhere?" a deep voice intoned.

My head jerked up, and I stared at Maverick Rivera. *Just great.* He was wearing jeans, a buttoned-up, black shirt, and his usual dark scowl.

"I'm going home," I said.

"You haven't even seen him, and you're leaving?"

Damn, I wasn't sure I had it in me to spar with Rivera right now. "They told me he was okay, but they wouldn't let me see him." My voice hitched. "He is okay, right?"

Maverick studied me, his gaze heavy and intense.

I grabbed the front of his shirt, half to make a point, and half to keep myself upright. "Rivera, is he all right?" Even I heard the panicked edge to my voice.

"He's fine."

I sagged. "Thank God." Then I straightened and locked my knees. I didn't want to show any weakness in front of this man. "I need to go."

He eyed my bare feet and arched a brow.

I felt a sudden spurt of anger. My head was throbbing now. "I tried to see him, but they told me he'd left instructions for no one to be let through. I got the message loud and clear."

Maverick's gaze shifted to my face. I felt a hot prick of tears and tried to push past him.

He grabbed my arm. "He's been in and out of consciousness. I gave the order to the front desk for him not to be disturbed, not him."

"Oh." I hunched my shoulders. I was really light-headed now. I needed to go because I was about to faint in front of Maverick.

I turned, weaving unsteadily.

"Aspen, shit, you're about to fall over."

Shocking the hell out of me, he scooped me into his arms.

I pressed a hand to his rock-hard chest. "Rivera, don't mess with me right now."

He stared down at me. "Liam rambled that you shoved him out of the way of a burning beam."

I didn't respond.

"And he carried you out of that burning building."

"He's a good man," I whispered. "The best."

"And you're just going to leave?"

"I'm...not exactly thinking clearly right now."

"I can see that." Maverick strode back into the hospital, carrying me in his arms.

"I'm not on my A-game, Rivera. I can't take you on right now."

His lips twitched. "I know. Save it for later."

"Where are you taking me?"

"To Liam."

Liam

Liam lunged off the bed and his vision blurred. "Where the hell is she?"

He was only wearing scrub bottoms, bandages covering the burns on his chest and arms.

Zane stepped forward. "Take it easy, Liam."

Monroe stood behind Zane, chewing on her lip, worry in her eyes.

"She was hurt." Liam coughed. Hell, his chest ached. "Where's Aspen? I need to be with her."

"The big guy, Boone, said you passed out, and they took her for treatment," Zane said.

"Find her, Zane." Liam pinned his friend with a glare.

"Okay, but only if you get back in bed."

"No." Liam tried to find his balance. "I'm not lying around while my woman is out there, probably wondering where the hell I am."

"Your woman?"

"She's *mine*." He met Zane's gaze. "I'm falling for her."

Monroe's laugh was low, and even though she might belong to his friend, Liam thought the sound was sexy.

"I *knew* it," she said.

"I need her." Liam raked a hand through his hair. "I need to know she's okay."

The door opened, and a panicked nurse and doctor rushed in.

The doctor frowned. "Mr. Kensington, you need to get back into bed—"

"No."

"You're suffering from smoke inhalation."

The door opened again, and Liam's heart leaped into his throat.

Mav shouldered in, with Aspen in his arms.

Liam surged forward. "Aspen—"

Her green gaze met his, then moved all over him, snagging on the bandages. "Liam."

Mav set her down, then she was in Liam's arms.

"*God*. Are you okay?" He yanked her hard against him. "I just woke up. I should've been with you."

"I'm okay... I... They wouldn't tell me where you were."

He hugged her tighter. She smelled like smoke, but she was alive.

"Mr. Kensington," the doctor tried again. "You need to get back into bed, and this lady needs to get back to her bed." The doctor looked at Aspen. "Did your attending doctor tell you that you could get out of bed?"

She stilled. "Um..."

"She's *not* going anywhere." Liam moved the few feet to the bed, and then urged Aspen up. He followed her in, stretched out, then pulled her against his side. She pressed her face to his chest and let out a sigh.

The doctor looked frustrated, blew out a breath, but finally left with the smiling nurse.

Liam pulled Aspen closer. "How badly are you hurt?"

"Minor burns. Smoke inhalation."

"Me too."

"Boone?" she asked.

"Is fine, but seriously doesn't like hospitals. I told him that I'd call once we were out. And Erica is with Jake. He's battered, but alive."

"Thank you." She lifted her gaze. "I heard Doyle's in surgery."

Zane shifted closer. "He might not make it. He's under guard."

"He... He told me he was responsible for the Ponzi scheme that my father was involved with."

Liam cursed.

She hugged him harder. "It doesn't matter. It's over now. He'll get what he deserves, whether he lives or not."

Liam's heart clenched. *Over.* Did she plan to walk away now that the case was done?

Her gaze shifted to the lockbox on the bedside table, and she gasped.

"*Liam.* You left a hundred and thirty million dollars' worth of treasure and priceless diamonds just sitting beside your hospital bed?"

Zane, Monroe, and Maverick sucked in collaborative breaths.

Liam tightened his arms. "It's not my priority."

He saw her face soften. "The photos?"

"Burned in the fire."

Monroe stepped over and flicked open the lockbox. She jerked. "Holy hell."

Liam and Aspen didn't even look.

Mav grunted. "I'll take it home with me and put it in my safe."

Liam saw Mav and Aspen share a look. Mav nodded, and Liam realized that sometime recently, his friend had changed his tune on Aspen.

"We'll let you guys get some rest." Zane patted Liam's arm. "Glad you're both okay."

Monroe leaned over and pressed a kiss to Liam's cheek. She smiled at Aspen.

"And I'm glad all this shit is over." Mav grabbed the lockbox and left.

After the door closed on his friends, Liam turned to face Aspen, feeling the sting of his wounds. He ignored the pain. "The case is over. The blackmail is over, but what isn't over, is us."

"Liam—"

"No, I don't want to hear you say we don't belong together. Being with you...you brought me to life, Aspen. Before, I was cruising, comfortable, bored, feeling I had to prove that I'm not like my father." He touched her cheek, trailed his finger down her cheekbone, then touched the dimple on her chin. "We fit. You make me laugh, think, feel. You're real, and I'd forgotten what real was."

"Liam—"

He pressed a finger to her lips. "We belong together, and I'm falling in love with you."

He heard her sharp intake of breath.

"And I know I've got a battle on my hands to convince you to be mine, but, darling, consider this a declaration of war."

"Liam," she said, firmly. "Can I talk now?"

He let his gaze trace over her face. "Very well."

"Thank you, your lordship."

He rolled his eyes.

"I..." She took a deep breath. "I'm falling for you, too."

"Aspen, you... Wait, what?" He'd expected an argument.

"You shouldn't be so surprised. I'm told you're a catch." She cupped his cheeks. "I don't care about your zillion-dollar condo, which needs more plants, by the way. Or your fancy cars. Or your sexy, hand-tailored suits. I care that you add color to my life. You see *me*. You trust my judgment. You ran into a burning warehouse to save me. Under the Armani, or Gucci, or whatever the hell you wear, you're my hero."

"*Aspen*." His voice was thick.

She smiled. "You don't have to fight to make me yours, because I already am. I think I have been for a while."

He slid a hand into her hair and kissed her.

A nurse strode in. "Well, I'm guessing you'll both have elevated heart rates. Now, time to unlock lips so I can check you both over."

Liam rubbed his nose against Aspen's and smiled.

20

MAKING IT OFFICIAL

Aspen

"Put out the pule, darling."

"Hell, no." I spun to face Liam. "I don't care if that cheese costs a fortune."

He was in what I called 'Liam casual'—pressed, tan pants and an untucked, white linen shirt.

Delicious.

I noted the bandage on the side of his neck and my belly tightened. I was so damn glad that we were alive and healing up every day.

What I felt for him, the love, grew bigger every day, too.

It had been a week since the warehouse fire and taking Nexus down.

We'd taken the week off—no work, no people, nothing but the two of us. We'd spent it all at his place having hot sex, watching movies, eating, sipping wine. We'd even sat by the fire pit on the terrace, huddled under a blanket together, watching the lights of the city.

Pure bliss.

Yes, I was falling more in love every day.

"Hey?" he said.

I looked up.

He moved in close and wrapped an arm around me. "I love you."

God, hearing him say that turned me to mush. Here it was—I'd danced around it by saying that I was falling for him. But the truth was that I was done falling and I'd hit the bottom.

It had been a scary fall, but I was all in. This man was *mine*.

I pressed my lips to his. "I love you too, Liam."

His eyes flared. "Good." Then he reached out and patted my butt. "Come on then, love of my life. We need to finish getting the food set out before our guests arrive."

Tonight, our friends and family were coming over for a party. We couldn't hold them off any longer, especially the twins. They bombarded me with texts every day. I watched as Liam set out a fancy board covered in cheese, crackers, and meats on the kitchen island. He swiveled, then came back carrying a huge tray of Belgian chocolates he'd bought just for me.

The man loved spoiling me.

The other thing we'd been doing this week was dodging the press.

I'd turned in everything I had on Nexus to the police, and the crime group was now in tatters. Since Liam was involved, the story had blown wide open. Doyle had survived his surgery but was in a coma. Jackie Godin and her cohorts were in jail.

I felt a savage spurt of satisfaction.

Everyone wanted to know about Dutch Schultz's treasure. Liam had donated it to the New-York Historical Society, and they were planning a huge exhibition.

The other piece of news that the press had lapped up was that the second billionaire bachelor of New York was off the market.

Liam had taken great delight in telling the world that he was in love with a beautiful, fascinating private investigator who'd gone undercover to blackmail a billionaire. We couldn't leave the penthouse without a pack of paparazzi following us. The papers were full of stories of the plucky, attractive investigator who'd stolen the heart of the billionaire. *Ugh.*

I scowled. Every time I looked online, I was confronted with a photo of myself. The damn reporters had interviewed everyone I knew—including Mrs. Kerber, Mr. Cavonis at the convenience store, hell, I think they'd even interviewed my high school English teacher.

The doorbell rang. Liam had already told the doormen to let the guests up.

"I'll get it," I called out.

I ran my hands down my white slacks. I'd paired it with a silky dark-blue shirt with a deep V neck. Liam's New York tailor had already left me a ton of messages about his 'vision' for my wardrobe.

I shuddered at the thought. This girlfriend of a billionaire thing was not easy.

I glanced over at him. He was popping the cork on a bottle of wine, and my gaze fell to the sharp line of his jaw.

It was *so* worth it.

As I walked to the door, I saw the plant that Liam had given me that morning. My insides melted. It rested in place of pride on the entry table. It was a gorgeous rose succulent in both pinks and greens, also known as Greenovia. I'd mentioned that I'd wanted one, and today he'd made it appear.

I opened the door and my insides turned to ice.

Rupert Kensington pushed inside.

"So, you're a private investigator, I hear." He didn't sound very happy about it.

"What are you doing here?" I asked coldly.

"Checking on my son and his gold digger." Liam's father sniffed. "He can do so much better."

I raised a brow. "I don't live up to your standards. Boo-hoo. I'm heartbroken." I kept my voice monotone.

Liam sauntered over. "Careful, father. Aspen will eviscerate you with utmost ease. And I'll enjoy watching."

Rupert turned to Liam, dismissing me. "I see you look fine."

Liam met my gaze. "He's here for two things. One, no doubt there are some photographers downstairs who caught some pictures of the *concerned* father coming to check on his son." Liam looked back at his father, his gaze hard. "Two, to ensure the pictures of him abusing teenage girls were destroyed."

Rupert bristled. "I try to be cordial. I have your best interests at heart. And all I get from you is rudeness."

"Save it, Father. A smart woman told me recently that our past is our past. We learn and move on. We can't let it drive us. You're my past. I'm nothing like you and I want nothing to do with you."

"Fine. You've always been selfish, self-important, and insolent."

I burst out laughing. "Seriously? There wasn't even a hint of irony as he said that."

Liam's lips twitched. "It sailed right over his head. He probably believes every word."

I shook my head. "Talk about projection."

Rupert scowled at us. "The photos?"

"Yes, here's the real reason for the visit from dear old dad. They're gone. Destroyed."

The older Kensington hesitated. "You're sure?"

"Yes, Father. Now go."

I studied Liam's face. I saw no sadness or anger. He looked disinterested, slightly bored. I smiled. "Let me get the door for you, Mr. Kensington."

With a haughty look, Rupert stepped out.

I took great pleasure in slamming the door behind him.

I moved over to Liam, and he wrapped his arms around me in a firm hug.

"I love a smart, kind, sexy, wonderful man," I said.

"And I love a smart, giving, sexy, wonderful woman." He rubbed his nose against mine. "Think we can both put the daddy issues away now?"

I nodded.

Then he lowered his head, his lips taking mine. *Mmm.*

I heard a beep and suddenly, the front door opened.

"Hey, this is a party, not a kiss-fest." Mav sauntered in, followed by Monroe and Zane.

"Party time," I said with a smile.

Liam

Liam sipped the whisky. Not bad. It was a forty-year-old Karuizawa single malt whisky. He preferred Scotch, but Japanese whisky this good was a nice change.

"Like it?" Mav asked.

"Superb."

"I figured I'd bring it to celebrate you not being dead, and not having to clean up a sex scandal."

Liam lifted his glass. "Cheers to that."

"And to celebrate you being in love."

Liam hadn't expected that to be something that Maverick Rivera would want to celebrate. "Thanks, Mav."

Scanning the room, Liam found Aspen. She was laughing with her mom, her sisters, and Monroe. One of the twins—Liam wasn't sure which—was waving her arms around and telling a story.

But his gaze was solely for Aspen. Damn, he loved her so much.

He'd called his mother and Annabelle to update them on the situation. He'd known that they'd probably get calls from reporters and read about what had happened in the press. Annabelle had been thrilled that he'd fallen in love and couldn't wait to meet Aspen. His mother was less pleased and more cautious.

He didn't care. He didn't need their approval.

Nearby, Liam spotted Jake Knox sitting in a chair. The bruises on the man's face were now ugly shades of green and yellow. But he was healing. Erica sat beside him, holding a soda and lime. The man reached out and rested a hand on his wife's still-flat belly.

The couple shared a private smile.

Then Jake looked up and met Liam's gaze. The man nodded.

Liam nodded back.

A few other friends were there, including Eleanor and her husband. Liam's assistant was sipping champagne, but she gave him the evil eye. Yes, she hadn't quite forgiven him for taking a week off at the last minute. She'd been the one who'd had to cancel and reschedule meetings, and soothe ruffled feathers.

Boone stood with Eleanor and her husband, cradling a bottle of beer. When he saw Liam looking, he lifted his bottle.

Liam lifted his glass in return. Without the man's help, Liam and Aspen might not have made it out alive.

Suddenly, Maverick muttered a curse.

He was glaring at his phone.

"Problem?" Zane asked.

"Over the last twenty-four hours, someone's been targeting the Rivera Tech system with some high-level cyber attacks."

Liam frowned. "Have they managed to get in?"

"No," Mav growled. "But they're having a good go at it. They're good, but not good enough. Rollo and I have been busy beefing up system security."

At the mention of her hacker friend, Monroe smiled and sipped her wine. "I've never seen Rollo happier. He loves working for Rivera Tech."

"Because I supplied him with a top-of-the-line, experimental Rivera Tech computer," Mav said.

Liam studied his friend's face. "You're worried about these attacks."

Mav shrugged a broad shoulder. "We get thousands of attacks a day, but these ones are more sophisticated. They haven't gotten in, but I worry that they aren't going to stop trying. If they can't get in, they'll find a better hacker who can."

"Makes you wonder what they're after?" Zane said.

Mav's scowl deepened.

"Mav," Liam said. "If anyone can stop this, it's you."

His friend looked at his phone again, his jaw hardening. "Hell, yeah. I'll stop them and make them regret it."

"Liam!"

Liam turned. One of the twins was waving at him. He was pretty sure it was Briar.

"When are you and my sister making it official?"

His fingers curled around his glass. He saw heat flood Aspen's face.

"Briar!" Aspen snapped.

Liam smiled. *Briar*. He'd been right.

"I mean her moving into your totally awesomesauce

pad," Briar continued. "She's slept here every night this week."

"*Briar*," Aspen said again.

Liam's smile widened. He walked toward his woman.

"Ignore her, Liam," Aspen said. "She's—"

He took Aspen's hand and pulled it flat against his chest. "Aspen, will you move in with me?"

She froze. Her mouth dropped open.

"Fill my place with plants. Drop your clothes on the bedroom floor. I'll buy you chocolates every day. Be mine, Aspen Chandler. Now and forever."

"*Liam*." Warmth filled her face and she melted against him.

His tough investigator melted just for him.

"Say yes," he whispered.

"Yes," she whispered back.

He grinned, scooped her off her feet, and kissed her. Their friends and family cheered.

What had started with blackmail, now ended with love, and Liam couldn't be happier.

I hope you enjoyed Aspen and Liam's story!

The **Billionaire Heists Trilogy** concludes with *Hacking Mr. CEO*, starring grumpy billionaire Maverick Rivera, releasing next month, on the 27th July 2021.

Want to know more about Vander Norcross? Then check out the first book in the Norcross Security series, *The*

Investigator, starring Vander's brother Rhys. **Read on for a preview of the first chapter.**

And for more on Declan Ward, Darcy Ward, and Special Agent Alastair Burke, then don't miss the **Treasure Hunter Security** series, which starts with Declan's story, *Undiscovered*.

Don't miss out! For updates about new releases, free books, and other fun stuff, sign up for my VIP mailing list and get your *free box set* containing three action-packed romances.

Visit here to get started: www.annahackett.com

Would you like a FREE BOX SET of my books?

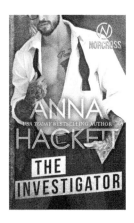

There was a glass of chardonnay with her name on it waiting for her at home.

Haven McKinney smiled. The museum was closed, and she was *done* for the day.

As she walked across the East gallery of the Hutton Museum, her heels clicked on the marble floor.

God, she loved the place. The creamy marble that made up the flooring and wrapped around the grand pillars was gorgeous. It had that hushed air of grandeur that made her heart squeeze a little every time she stepped inside. But more than that, the amazing art the Hutton housed sang to the art lover in her blood.

Snagging a job here as the curator six months ago had been a dream come true. She'd been at a low point in her life. Very low. Haven swallowed a snort and circled a stunning white-marble sculpture of a naked, reclining woman with the most perfect resting bitch face. She'd never guessed that her life would come crashing down at age twenty-nine.

She lifted her chin. Miami was her past. The Hutton and San Francisco were her future. No more throwing caution to the wind. She had a plan, and she was sticking to it.

She paused in front of a stunning exhibit of traditional Chinese painting and calligraphy. It was one of their newer exhibits, and had been Haven's brainchild. Nearby, an interactive display was partially assembled. Over the next few days, her staff would finish the installation. Excitement zipped through Haven. She couldn't wait to have the touchscreens operational. It was her passion to make art more accessible, especially to children. To help them be a part of it, not just look at it. To learn, to feel, to enjoy.

Art had helped her through some of the toughest times in her life, and she wanted to share that with others.

She looked at the gorgeous old paintings again. One portrayed a mountainous landscape with beautiful maple trees. It soothed her nerves.

Wine would soothe her nerves, as well. *Right.* She

needed to get upstairs to her office and grab her handbag, then get an Uber home.

Her cell phone rang and she unclipped it from the lanyard she wore at the museum. "Hello?"

"Change of plans, girlfriend," a smoky female voice said. "Let's go out and celebrate being gorgeous, successful, and single. I'm done at the office, and believe me, it has been a *grueling* day."

Haven smiled at her new best friend. She'd met Gia Norcross when she joined the Hutton. Gia's wealthy brother, Easton Norcross, owned the museum, and was Haven's boss. The museum was just a small asset in the businessman's empire. Haven suspected Easton owned at least a third of San Francisco. Maybe half.

She liked and respected her boss. Easton could be tough, but he valued her opinions. And she loved his bossy, take-charge, energetic sister. Gia ran a highly successful PR firm in the city, and did all the PR and advertising for the Hutton. They'd met not long after Haven had started work at the museum.

After their first meeting, Gia had dragged Haven out to her favorite restaurant and bar, and the rest was history.

"I guess making people's Instagram look pretty and not staged is hard work," Haven said with a grin.

"Bitch." Gia laughed. "God, I had a meeting with a businessman caught in...well, let's just say he and his assistant were *not* taking notes on the boardroom table."

Haven felt an old, unwelcome memory rise up. She mentally stomped it down. "I don't feel sorry for the cheating asshole, I feel sorry for whatever poor shmuck got more than they were paid for when they walked into the boardroom."

"Actually, it was the cheating businessman's wife."

"Uh-oh."

"And the assistant was male," Gia added.

"Double uh-oh."

"Then said cheater comes to my PR firm, telling me to clean up his mess, because he's thinking he might run for governor one day. I mean, I'm good, but I can't wrangle miracles."

Haven suspected that Gia had verbally eviscerated the man and sent him on his way. Gia Norcross had a sharp tongue, and wasn't afraid to use it.

"So, grueling day and I need alcohol. I'll meet you at ONE65, and the first drink is on me."

"I'm pretty wiped, Gia—"

"Uh-uh, no excuses. I'll see you in an hour." And with that, Gia was gone.

Haven clipped her phone to her lanyard. Well, it looked like she was having that chardonnay at ONE65, the six-story, French dining experience Gia loved. Each level offered something different, from patisserie, to bistro and grill, to bar and lounge.

Haven walked into the museum's main gallery, and her blood pressure dropped to a more normal level. It was her favorite space in the museum. The smell of wood, the gorgeous lights gleaming overhead, and the amazing paintings combined to create a soothing room. She smoothed her hands down her fitted, black skirt. Haven was tall, at five foot eight, and curvy, just like her mom had been. Her boobs, currently covered by a cute, white blouse with a tie around her neck, weren't much to write home about, but she had to buy her skirts one size bigger. She sighed. No matter how much she walked or jogged —*blergh*, okay, she didn't jog much—she still had an ass.

Even in her last couple of months in Miami, when stress had caused her to lose a bunch of weight due to everything going on, her ass hadn't budged.

Memories of Miami—and her douchebag-of-epic-proportions-ex—threatened, churning like storm clouds on the horizon.

Nope. She locked those thoughts down. She was *not* going there.

She had a plan, and the number one thing for taking back and rebuilding her life was *no* men. She'd sworn off anyone with a Y chromosome.

She didn't need one, didn't want one, she was D-O-N-E, done.

She stopped in front of the museum's star attraction. Claude Monet's *Water Lilies*.

Haven loved the impressionist's work. She loved the colors, the delicate strokes. This one depicted water lilies and lily pads floating on a gentle pond. His paintings always made an impact, and had a haunting, yet soothing feel to them.

It was also worth just over a hundred million dollars.

The price tag still made her heart flutter. She'd put a business case to Easton, and they'd purchased the painting three weeks ago at auction. Haven had planned out the display down to the rivets used on the wood. She'd thrown herself into the project.

Gia had put together a killer marketing campaign,

and Haven had reluctantly been interviewed by the local paper. But it had paid off. Ticket sales to the museum were up, and everyone wanted to see *Water Lilies*.

Footsteps echoed through the empty museum, and she turned to see a uniformed security guard appear in the doorway.

"Ms. McKinney?"

"Yes, David? I was just getting ready to leave."

"Sorry to delay you. There's a delivery truck at the back entrance. They say they have a delivery of a Zadkine bronze."

Haven frowned, running through the next day's schedule in her head. "That's due tomorrow."

"It sounds like they had some other deliveries nearby and thought they'd squeeze it in."

She glanced at her slim, silver wristwatch, fighting back annoyance. She'd had a long day, and now she'd be late to meet Gia. "Fine. Have them bring it in."

With a nod, David disappeared. Haven pulled out her phone and quickly fired off a text to warn Gia that she'd be late. Then Haven headed up to her office, and checked her notes for tomorrow. She had several calls to make to chase down some pieces for a new exhibit she wanted to launch in the winter. There were some restoration quotes to go over, and a charity gala for her art charity to plan. She needed to get down into the storage rooms and see if there was anything they could cycle out and put on display.

God, she loved her job. Not many people would get excited about digging around in dusty storage rooms, but Haven couldn't wait.

She made sure her laptop was off and grabbed her handbag. She slipped her lanyard off and stuffed her phone in her bag.

When she reached the bottom of the stairs, she heard a strange noise from the gallery. A muffled pop, then a thump.

Frowning, she took one step toward the gallery.

Suddenly, David staggered through the doorway, a splotch of red on his shirt.

Haven's pulse spiked. *Oh God, was that blood?* "David—"

"Run." He collapsed to the floor.

Fear choking her, she kicked off her heels and spun. She had to get help.

But she'd only taken two steps when a hand sank into her hair, pulling her neat twist loose, and sending her brown hair cascading over her shoulders.

"Let me go!"

She was dragged into the main gallery, and when she lifted her head, her gut churned.

Five men dressed in black, all wearing balaclavas, stood in a small group.

No...oh, no.

Their other guard, Gus, stood with his hands in the air. He was older, former military. She was shoved closer toward him.

"Ms. McKinney, you okay?" Gus asked.

She managed a nod. "They shot David."

"I kn—"

"No talking," one man growled.

Haven lifted her chin. "What do you want?" There was a slight quaver in her voice.

The man who'd grabbed her glared. His cold, blue eyes glittered through the slits in his balaclava. Then he ignored her, and with the others, they turned to face the *Water Lilies*.

Haven's stomach dropped. *No.* This couldn't be happening.

A thin man moved forward, studying the painting's gilt frame with gloved hands. "It's wired to an alarm."

Blue Eyes, clearly the group's leader, turned and aimed the gun at Gus' barrel chest. "Disconnect it."

"No," the guard said belligerently.

"I'm not asking."

Haven held up her hands. "Please—"

The gun fired. Gus dropped to one knee, pressing a hand to his shoulder.

"No!" she cried.

The leader stepped forward and pressed the gun to the older man's head.

"No." Haven fought back her fear and panic. "Don't hurt him. I'll disconnect it."

Slowly, she inched toward the painting, carefully avoiding the thin man still standing close to it. She touched the security panel built in beside the frame, pressing her palm to the small pad.

A second later, there was a discreet beep.

Two other men came forward and grabbed the frame.

She glanced around at them. "You're making a mistake. If you know who owns this museum, then you know you won't get away with this." Who would go up against the Norcross family? Easton, rich as sin, had a lot of connections, but his brother, Vander... Haven suppressed a shiver. Gia's middle brother might be hot, but he scared the bejesus out of Haven.

Vander Norcross, former military badass, owned Norcross Security and Investigations. His team had put in the high-tech security for the museum.

No one in their right mind wanted to go up against Vander, or the third Norcross brother who also worked with Vander, or the rest of Vander's team of badasses.

"Look, if you just—"

The blow to her head made her stagger. She blinked, pain radiating through her face. Blue Eyes had backhanded her.

He moved in and hit her again, and Haven cried out, clutching her face. It wasn't the first time she'd been hit. Her douchebag ex had hit her once. That was the day she'd left him for good.

But this was worse. Way worse.

"Shut up, you stupid bitch."

The next blow sent her to the floor. She thought she heard someone chuckle. He followed with a kick to her ribs, and Haven curled into a ball, a sob in her throat.

Her vision wavered and she blinked. Blue Eyes crouched down, putting his hand to the tiles right in front of her. Dizziness hit her, and she vaguely took in the freckles on the man's hand. They formed a spiral pattern.

"No one talks back to me," the man growled. "Especially a woman." He moved away.

She saw the men were busy maneuvering the painting off the wall. It was easy for two people to move.

She knew its exact dimensions—eighty by one hundred centimeters.

No one was paying any attention to her. Fighting through the nausea and dizziness, she dragged herself a few inches across the floor, closer to the nearby pillar. A pillar that had one of several hidden, high-tech panic buttons built into it.

When the men were turned away, she reached up and pressed the button.

Then blackness sucked her under.

HAVEN SAT on one of the lovely wooden benches she'd had installed around the museum. She'd wanted somewhere for guests to sit and take in the art.

She'd never expected to be sitting on one, holding a melting ice pack to her throbbing face, and staring at the empty wall where a multi-million-dollar masterpiece should be hanging. And she definitely didn't expect to be doing it with police dusting black powder all over the museum's walls.

Tears pricked her eyes. She was alive, her guards were hurt but alive, and that was what mattered. The police had questioned her and she'd told them everything she could remember. The paramedics had checked her over and given her the ice pack. Nothing was broken, but she'd been told to expect swelling and bruising.

David and Gus had been taken to the hospital. She'd been assured the men would be okay. Last she'd heard, David was in surgery. Her throat tightened. *Oh, God.*

What was she going to tell Easton?

Haven bit her lip and a tear fell down her cheek. She hadn't cried in months. She'd shed more than enough tears over Leo after he'd gone crazy and hit her. She'd left Miami the next day. She'd needed to get away from her ex and, unfortunately, despite loving her job at a classy Miami art gallery, Leo's cousin had owned it. Alyssa had been the one who had introduced them.

Haven had learned a painful lesson to not mix business and pleasure.

She'd been done with Leo's growing moodiness, outbursts, and cheating on her and hitting her had been the last straw. *Asshole.*

She wiped the tear away. San Francisco was as far from Miami as she could get and still be in the continental US. This was supposed to be her fresh new start.

She heard footsteps—solid, quick, and purposeful. Easton strode in.

He was a tall man, with dark hair that curled at the collar of his perfectly fitted suit. Haven had sworn off men, but she was still woman enough to appreciate her boss' good looks. His mother was Italian-American, and she'd passed down her very good genes to her children.

Like his brothers, Easton had been in the military, too, although he'd joined the Army Rangers. It showed in his muscled body. Once, she'd seen his shirt sleeves rolled up when they'd had a late meeting. He had some interesting ink that was totally at odds with his sophisticated-businessman persona.

His gaze swept the room, his jaw tight. It settled on her and he strode over.

"Haven—"

"Oh God, Easton. I'm so sorry."

He sat beside her and took her free hand. He squeezed her cold fingers, then he looked at her face and cursed.

She hadn't been brave enough to look in the mirror, but she guessed it was bad.

"They took the *Water Lilies*," she said.

"Okay, don't worry about it just now."

She gave a hiccupping laugh. "Don't worry? It's worth a hundred and ten *million* dollars."

A muscle ticked in his jaw. "You're okay, and that's the main thing. And the guards are in serious but stable condition at the hospital."

She nodded numbly. "It's all my fault."

Easton's gaze went to the police, and then moved back to her. "That's not true."

"I let them in." Her voice broke. God, she wanted the marble floor to crack and swallow her.

"Don't worry." Easton's face turned very serious. "Vander and Rhys will find the painting."

Her boss' tone made her shiver. Something made her suspect that Easton wanted his brothers to find the men who'd stolen the painting more than recovering the priceless piece of art.

She licked her lips, and felt the skin on her cheek tug. She'd have some spectacular bruises later. *Great. Thanks, universe.*

Then Easton's head jerked up, and Haven followed his gaze.

A man stood in the doorway. She hadn't heard him

coming. Nope, Vander Norcross moved silently, like a ghost.

He was a few inches over six feet, had a powerful body, and radiated authority. His suit didn't do much to tone down the sense that a predator had stalked into the room. While Easton was handsome, Vander wasn't. His face was too rugged, and while both he and Easton had blue eyes, Vander's were dark indigo, and as cold as the deepest ocean depths.

He didn't look happy. She fought back a shiver.

Then another man stepped up beside Vander.

Haven's chest locked. *Oh, no. No, no, no.*

She should have known. He was Vander's top investigator. Rhys Matteo Norcross, the youngest of the Norcross brothers.

At first glance, he looked like his brothers—similar build, muscular body, dark hair and bronze skin. But Rhys was the youngest, and he had a charming edge his brothers didn't share. He smiled more frequently, and his shaggy, thick hair always made her imagine him as a rock star, holding a guitar and making girls scream.

Haven was also totally, one hundred percent in lust with him. Any time he got near, he made her body flare to life, her heart beat faster, and made her brain freeze up. She could barely talk around the man.

She did *not* want Rhys Norcross to notice her. Or talk to her. Or turn his soulful, brown eyes her way.

Nuh-uh. No way. She'd sworn off men. This one should have a giant warning sign hanging on him. *Watch out, heartbreak waiting to happen.*

Rhys had been in the military with Vander. Some

hush-hush special unit that no one talked about. Now he worked at Norcross Security—apparently finding anything and anyone.

He also raced cars and boats in his free time. The man liked to go fast. Oh, and he bedded women. His reputation was legendary. Rhys liked a variety of adventures and experiences.

It was lucky Haven had sworn off men.

Especially when they happened to be her boss' brother.

And especially, especially when they were also her best friend's brother.

Off limits.

She saw the pair turn to look her and Easton's way.

Crap. Pulse racing, she looked at her bare feet and red toenails, which made her realize she hadn't recovered her shoes yet. They were her favorites.

She felt the men looking at her, and like she was drawn by a magnet, she looked up. Vander was scowling. Rhys' dark gaze was locked on her.

Haven's traitorous heart did a little tango in her chest.

Before she knew what was happening, Rhys went down on one knee in front of her.

She saw rage twist his handsome features. Then he shocked her by cupping her jaw, and pushing the ice pack away.

They'd never talked much. At Gia's parties, Haven purposely avoided him. He'd never touched her before, and she felt the warmth of him singe through her.

His eyes flashed. "It's going to be okay, baby."

Baby?

He stroked her cheekbone, those long fingers gentle.

Fighting for some control, Haven closed her hand over his wrist. She swallowed. "I—"

"Don't worry, Haven. I'm going to find the man who did this to you and make him regret it."

Her belly tightened. *Oh, God.* When was the last time anyone had looked out for her like this? She was certain no one had ever promised to hunt anyone down for her. Her gaze dropped to his lips.

He had amazingly shaped lips, a little fuller than such a tough man should have, framed by dark stubble.

There was a shift in his eyes and his face warmed. His fingers kept stroking her skin and she felt that caress all over.

Then she heard the click of heels moving at speed. Gia burst into the room.

"What the hell is going on?"

Haven jerked back from Rhys and his hypnotic touch. Damn, she'd been proven right—she was so weak where this man was concerned.

Gia hurried toward them. She was five-foot-four, with a curvy, little body, and a mass of dark, curly hair. As usual, she wore one of her power suits—short skirt, fitted jacket, and sky-high heels.

"Out of my way." Gia shouldered Rhys aside. When her friend got a look at Haven, her mouth twisted. "I'm going to *kill* them."

"Gia," Vander said. "The place is filled with cops. Maybe keep your plans for murder and vengeance quiet."

"Fix this." She pointed at Vander's chest, then at

Rhys. Then she turned and hugged Haven. "You're coming home with me."

"Gia—"

"No. No arguments." Gia held up her palm like a traffic cop. Haven had seen "the hand" before. It was pointless arguing.

Besides, she realized she didn't want to be alone. And the quicker she got away from Rhys' dark, far-too-perceptive gaze, the better.

Norcross Security
The Investigator
The Troubleshooter
The Specialist
The Bodyguard

W ant to learn more about the mysterious, covert
Team 52? Check out the first book in the series,
Mission: Her Protection.

**When Rowan's Arctic research team pulls
a strange object out of the ice in Northern**

Canada, things start to go wrong...very, very wrong. Rescued by a covert, black ops team, she finds herself in the powerful arms of a man with scary gold eyes. A man who vows to do everything and anything to protect her...

Dr. Rowan Schafer has learned it's best to do things herself and not depend on anyone else. Her cold, academic parents taught her that lesson. She loves the challenge of running a research base, until the day her scientists discover the object in a retreating glacier. Under attack, Rowan finds herself fighting to survive... until the mysterious Team 52 arrives.

Former special forces Marine Lachlan Hunter's military career ended in blood and screams, until he was recruited to lead a special team. A team tasked with a top-secret mission—to secure and safeguard pieces of powerful ancient technology. Married to his job, he's done too much and seen too much to risk inflicting his demons on a woman. But when his team arrives in the Arctic, he uncovers both an unexplained artifact, and a young girl from his past, now all grown up. A woman who ignites emotions inside him like never before.

But as Team 52 heads back to their base in Nevada, other hostile forces are after the artifact. Rowan finds herself under attack, and as the bullets fly, Lachlan vows to protect her at all costs. But in the face of danger like they've never seen before, will it be enough to keep her alive.

Team 52
Mission: Her Protection
Mission: Her Rescue
Mission: Her Security
Mission: Her Defense
Mission: Her Safety
Mission: Her Freedom
Mission: Her Shield
Also Available as Audiobooks!

Want to learn more about *Treasure Hunter Security*? Check out the first book in the series, *Undiscovered*, Declan Ward's action-packed story.

One former Navy SEAL. One dedicated archeologist. One secret map to a fabulous lost oasis.

Finding undiscovered treasures is always daring, dangerous, and deadly. Perfect for the men of Treasure Hunter Security. Former Navy SEAL Declan Ward is haunted by the demons of his past and throws everything he has into his security business—Treasure Hunter Security. Dangerous archeological digs – no problem. Daring expeditions – sure thing. Museum security for invaluable exhibits – easy. But on a simple dig in the Egyptian desert, he collides with a stubborn, smart archeologist, Dr. Layne Rush, and together they get swept into a deadly treasure hunt for a mythical lost oasis. When an evil from his past reappears, Declan vows to do anything to protect Layne.

Dr. Layne Rush is dedicated to building a successful career—a promise to the parents she lost far too young. But when her dig is plagued by strange accidents, targeted by a lethal black market antiquities ring, and artifacts are stolen, she is forced to turn to Treasure Hunter Security, and to the tough, sexy, and too-used-to-giving-orders Declan. Soon her organized dig morphs into a wild treasure hunt across the desert dunes.

Danger is hunting them every step of the way, and Layne and Declan must find a way to work together...to not only find the treasure but to survive.

Treasure Hunter Security
Undiscovered
Uncharted
Unexplored
Unfathomed

Untraveled
Unmapped
Unidentified
Undetected
Also Available as Audiobooks!

Undiscovered

Uncharted

Unexplored

Unfathomed

Untraveled

Unmapped

Unidentified

Undetected

Also Available as Audiobooks!

Eon Warriors

Edge of Eon

Touch of Eon

Heart of Eon

Kiss of Eon

Mark of Eon

Claim of Eon

Storm of Eon

Soul of Eon

Also Available as Audiobooks!

Galactic Gladiators: House of Rone

Sentinel

Defender

Centurion

Paladin

Guard

Weapons Master

Also Available as Audiobooks!

Galactic Gladiators

Gladiator

Warrior

Hero

Protector

Champion

Barbarian

Beast

Rogue

Guardian

Cyborg

Imperator

Hunter

Also Available as Audiobooks!

Hell Squad

Marcus

Cruz

Gabe

Reed

Roth

Noah

Shaw

Holmes

Niko

Finn

Devlin

Theron

Hemi

Ash

Levi

Manu

Griff

Dom

Survivors

Tane

Also Available as Audiobooks!

The Anomaly Series

Time Thief

Mind Raider

Soul Stealer

Salvation

Anomaly Series Box Set